SCREAM,
MY DARLING,
SCREAM! by
angela pearson

SCREAM, MY DARLING, SCREAM! by angela pearson

DELECTUS
London

First published in 1963.

This facsimile edition is published by
Delectus
27 Old Gloucester Street
London
WC1N 3XX

Copyright © Delectus 1998
Cover photograph © Irina Ionesco

All rights reserved.

No part of this book may be reproduced, stored in a retrieval system, or transmitted in any form, by any means, including mechanical, electronic, photocopying, recording or otherwise, without prior written permission from the publisher, in accordance with the provisions of the Copyright Act 1956 (as amended).

ISBN: 1 897767 16 1

Cover design and additional typesetting by Image Engineering.

Printed by Woolnough Ltd.,
Irthlingborough, Northamptonshire.

CONTENTS

I. I Don't Suppose You'll Kill Me. 7

II. A Potentially Dangerous Situation. 23

III. A Little Music While You Work. 37

IV. It's Time For Your Morning Caning. 67

V. Guilty of Objectionable Behaviour. 85

VI. Scream, My Darling, Scream! 135

I

I DON'T SUPPOSE YOU'LL KILL ME

Because it was a matinee performance the cinema was half empty.
The man and the girl sat in an oasis of vacant seats at the back of the dress-circle. They sat back in their seats, seemingly relaxed and absorbed in the film. A casual observer might have thought they were husband and wife, or brother and sister, or friends. No one would have taken them for lovers. No one could have suspected what the girl's right hand was doing, and no one would have guessed that, as a result of what her hand was doing, the man was tense and trembling.
An hour before, he had zipped open his flies hutched his penis out of his pants and trousers, and felt for the girl's hand. He had drawn it on to his lap. Unhesitatingly her fingers gripped the penis. It grew huge under her touch. She began to caress it and squeeze it alternately.
The background music changed its tempo and began to signal the beginning of the end of the film. She

gave another squeeze and then a little slap. She drew her hand back to her lap. He shifted slightly in his seat and pulled his penis back into his trousers and pants. "Thank you," he said quietly, as he zipped his flies shut. "That was extremely nice."

"Not at all," she murmured.

"Thank God it's nearly over. I want to get you home."

"Didn't you enjoy it?"

"How could I pay attention to a film—with you doing that?"

She laughed. "Pity. It was a very good film."

As they went down the stairs to the foyer, the assistant manager saw the girl and caught his breath sharply. He stared wide-eyed for a moment and then turned to speak through a half-open door. "Tom, come here. If you want to see a really lovely chicken, just come out here for a mo'."

The manager appeared in the doorway. "Where?"

"Coming down the stairs."

The manager whistled softly. "Wow!" he said.

"I'd give a lot to be in that chap's shoes."

"I'd give a month's pay myself."

"And it'd be cheap." The assistant manager gave a resigned sigh. "Oh well, some people have all the luck."

Unaware of the comments they were occasioning, the man and the girl crossed the foyer, went down the wide steps and turned into the car-park.

Having started the engine, the man felt again for the girl's hand and made to unzip his flies.

She shook her head. "Not while you're driving, Peter."

"Let's get home quickly then."

"For more love-making?"

He grinned. "Of course for more love-making."

"You're insatiable."

"Where you're concerned—yes, I'm insatiable."

She hesitated. "I'm not all sure that we can."
"Oh, I see." He tried to hide the disappointment in his voice. "Your period?"
"No. That's not for another week or so."
He glanced at her. "What then? Why can't we?"
She studied her gloved fingers for a moment. "You very much want to?"
"That is a silly question."
"I wonder *how* much you want to."
"You're being very mysterious. What's on your mind?"
"I have a condition."
"What condition? What do you mean?"
"I mean that we can make love again if you fulfil just one condition first."
He glanced at her again, his eyebrows raised. "What condition?"
She drew a breath before replying. "That I give you a whipping first."
"A *whipping!*" He turned his head and stared at her.
"Yes, Peter dear. A whipping. But don't look at your passenger. Look at the road."
He was silent for a long moment. "So you're a sadist," he said in a flat voice. "Well, well."
"I'm not absolutely sure. I think I am, though."
"Don't you know? If you want to whip me, I should've thought it would be pretty clear."
She put a hand on his knee and patted it affectionately. "I want to try it out."
"You've never done it before?"
"No. But I've often wanted to. Ever since I was a child. At school I used to dream of tying the history master to a tree and flogging him with a cat-o'-nine-tails. Naked, of course."
He drew a long breath. "I see. And now the moment has come. With me."
"Yes. With you. If you agree. But it depends on how much you want to make love to me."

"I think I need a drink."

She laughed at his woeful tone. "Poor Peter."

Despite himself, he laughed with her. "You are an awful bitch."

The momentary tension had broken. "Let's go to your flat anyway," she said. "You can have your drink. And in the meantime you can be thinking it over."

Twenty minutes later, having downed a large whisky and soda, he said: "One thing I don't understand. We've made love five or six times and you've never brought this up. Why? I mean, why haven't you even mentioned it?"

"That's very easy to answer. Shyness. It isn't a very easy thing to bring up, you know."

He grinned. "I think I can agree with you."

"But the time *has* come," she went on grimly. "I simply must try my hand at it, and find out."

"Find out whether you're a sadist or not?"

"Exactly. If I like it, I'm a sadist—and you'll have to decide what to do. If I don't like it, I'm not a sadist—but there's not much harm done."

He snorted. "Except that I've had a whipping that I haven't done anything to deserve."

She looked at him reflectively. "Yes, Peter. That's how it is. I simply must deliver a whipping, to find out. I'd rather it were you I give it to, but if you're not willing to take it I'll wait till I find someone else who is."

"I see," he said, and got up from the sofa. "I want another drink. You sure you won't have one?"

"I will now, please."

"What would you like?"

"Sherry, if there's any left."

He held up the bottle. "Yes, plenty."

She waited till he had brought the glasses. "Well, Peter?"

He drank deeply from his glass, his eyes on hers.

He put it down on the table and sighed. "All right. I don't suppose you'll kill me."

She smiled happily and threw her arms around his neck. "You're a darling! And I won't kill you, don't worry. I'll just tie you up and give you a bitsy little whipping."

"What are you going to do it with?"

"A whip, of course."

"When?"

"Now. Before we make love."

"But where are you going to find a whip. There certainly isn't one in this flat."

She smiled silkily. "Yes, there is. There's one in my bag. Open it and see."

He stared at her. "You carry a whip around with you?"

She looked back into his eyes and began to laugh helplessly at the expression of outrage that she read in them. "No, not usually, Peter," she said, when she had recovered herself. "Only since this morning. I bought one before lunch."

"To use on *me?*"

"I hoped I would be able to persuade you to let me."

"My God!" he said. "Saturday afternoon activities. What next?"

"Don't you want to see it?"

"I'm not so sure that I do."

"You will sooner or later."

"The later the better."

She laughed again. "Come on, now. Look in my bag."

He leaned forward and picked up her large brown crocodile handbag. He gave it to her.

She shook her head. "You take it out."

He opened the catch and put his hand inside. He felt the whip at once. He pulled it out of the bag. It was in a coil. He straightened it. He felt a little cold as he looked at it. It was a very cruel-looking instrument.

It had a leather-covered handle about six inches long. The lash, of tightly pleated leather, was about eighteen inches long. At the handle end it was of about the thickness of a finger. It tapered down to about half this thickness before it reached its tip.

Speechlessly, he sat looking at it in his hands.

She leaned forward and took it from him. She took the handle in her right hand and ran the lash lovingly through the fingers of her left. "It's such a lovely little whip, isn't it?" She pictured herself whipping his naked body with it. She began to breathe faster, her pulses drumming inside her. "Look again in the bag. See what else is there."

He obeyed her without a word. At the bottom of the bag he found a small ball of stout twine. He gave it to her.

She said, smiling sweetly at him: "You can imagine what this is for, can't you?"

He forced himself to smile back at her. "Yes, but is it necessary to tie me up? I've agreed to take a whipping from you. Isn't that enough?"

"No," she said forcefully. "I don't really think that is quite enough. You might change your mind. You'd better be properly tied up."

"Where are you going to do it?"

"In your bedroom."

"On the bed?"

"Yes. Your hands and legs are going to be tied to the four corners of the bed."

"Christ!" He got up. "I need another drink."

"All right. But only one more, Peter. You're going to make love to me afterwards. I don't want a drunken lover."

When he had poured his whisky and downed it at a gulp, she said, "The time has come, my Peter." She got up from the sofa, running the lash through the fingers of her left hand. Her heart was pounding almost painfully. The time had come at last.

She had told Peter that she had dreamed of flogging her history master with a cat-o'-nine-tails. But she had left it there. Despite her new-found determination not to be ashamed of her unusual desires (which didn't seem to her to be so unusual after all), she was still a little too shy to tell him more. She could have told him that she had once, at the age of thirteen, fought with a boy of twelve and had utterly mastered him. He had submitted to the indignity of kissing her feet, in order to avoid more blows. But what she wanted more than anything else in the world, at that moment, was to lay a whip across his back and legs. She had been too young to think of whipping him without his clothes; simply to whip him and make him scream would have been more than enough.

She had never wanted to whip anyone of her own sex. And she had never wanted to whip any man who did not attract her. Because of her beauty, she had received a good deal of attention for as long as she could remember from men of all ages. Most of this attention had left her cold; some of it had irritated, even angered, her. She had never wanted to punish it with a whip. But when a man attracted her, she would picture him naked, tied to a tree, helpless, screaming under her whip. And then, having reduced him to a condition of terrified, abject, servitude, she would picture herself reviving him with her kisses and her caresses. And he would make love to her. And then she would whip him again, to remind him that he was the slave. She would reduce him again to the condition of abject servitude.

But these had remained day-dreams all these years. There had been, as far as she could see, no way of fulfilling them. It had seemed so—so unthinkable, so unnatural, to tell a man that she wanted to whip him, to make a slave of him.

Now, however, her time had come at last.

"Get yourself stripped, Peter," she said. She swung the whip through the air. It sang ominously. She swung it harder, viciously. It hissed.

Peter swallowed. "Look, Susan. Perhaps, after all, we'd better call this off."

She regarded him coldly. The moment was a little dangerous. If he slipped out of her fingers now, if he refused after all to submit to her, she would have to return to her day-dreams and her frustrated longings. For a second she wondered whether she should cajole him, or appeal to his manhood, or simply give him orders. She chose the latter course.

"It's too late to call it off," she said, with the crisp snap of authority in her voice. "Get your clothes off at once. Go on, do as I say." For a moment she considered giving him a lash across his shoulders, but she thought better of it. She must get him safely tied to the four corners of the bed first.

He looked into her eyes and saw her determination. He tried to out-stare her but found that her will was stronger than his. He dropped his eyes. He began to undress himself.

Susan felt weak for a moment. It had been a near thing. She wondered what she would have done if he had told her to go to hell. But now he was undressing. Everything was going to be all right. She had won the battle of wills.

"Go into your bedroom," she ordered, coiling the whip in her hands.

She took the eiderdown off the bed and put it on a chair. "This will be in the way."

He said without interest: "It might have been nice to lie on." He was only making conversation. His thoughts were whirling round in his mind, confusing him. Something told him to stop this dangerous game before it went any further. But something else—perhaps the memory of the steel-like determination in her eyes—drove him on and made him continue to undress. And then he asked himself why he was being so obedient. Did he want *so* much to make love to her? There were other girls, for God's sake, weren't there? And other girls—not so lovely, of course; no one could be so lovely as Susan—would not want to give him a whipping. A *whipping*, for Christ's sake! With that dreadful, snaky-looking whip...

"Look, Susan," he said again. "I think——"

"I *am* looking," she replied coldly. "And I see you are taking the devil of a time to get stripped. Come on, *hurry!*"

Her tone drove away his last resistance. Without looking at her, he pulled off his socks, slipped his pants down over his feet, and stood naked.

"At last," she said. "Now lie down on the bed. And stretch your hands and legs to the four corners."

He did as she ordered, allowing himself only a tremulous sigh as she came with the twine in her hands and tied one of his wrists to the corner of the bed.

"I need a knife," she said. "Or scissors. I want to cut this string."

"There are scissors on the dressing-table," he muttered.

When she had tied his other wrist and both his feet she stood back and looked at him. Her heart was beating so fast that it was almost painful. At last a man was in her power, at her mercy. She could do to him what she wanted. She could give him ten lashes, or she could whip him for ten hours. She could even kill him with her whip if she wanted. She could flog him slowly to death.

She gave herself a mental shake. She had better stop such thoughts, she told herself. Let it be sufficient that she could at last give a man a simple whipping.

"How many lashes are you going to give me?" he asked, twisting his head to look at her. She was standing beside the bed, the whip dangling from her right hand. Her left hand was cupped over one of her breasts.

"I don't know yet," she said breathlessly.

"Not more than six, anyway, I hope."

"Six!" She laughed pityingly at the silliness of the number. "Six, you say! My dear Peter, this is not a visit to the headmaster for six of the best. This is *sexual,* don't you understand? It's going to be a full-scale sexual flagellation." *Sexual flagellation,* she repeated silently to herself, and felt a strong thrill at the words. She suddenly realised that her sexual juices had begun to wet the lips of her vagina. She put her free hand down and pressed it. A sweet ache filled her loins. "Six!" she repeated scornfully. "Let's say sixty—at any rate to begin with. Then we'll see."

"Sixty!" he exploded. "For God's sake, you'll kill me."

"No," she said sweetly. "I promise to stop before I kill you."

He glared at her. His glare was compounded more of terror than anger. He saw again the steely determination in her eyes. With a sickly feeling of despair he realised fully how much he was at her mercy. He turned his head and buried his face into the pillow. He cursed silently at his stupidity. How could he ever have been such an idiot as to get himself into such a position. "Oh Christ! Oh God!" he muttered between gritted teeth. Suddenly a frightening thought occurred to him. He twisted his head again. She was regarding his naked body with the light of some unearthly passion in her eyes. She was beginning to raise the whip above her head. "Stop a moment!" he said urgently.

"What is it now?" She let her whip fall to her side.

"You're not going to put that thing across my back, are you? You're going to whip my bottom, aren't you?"

She moistened her lips. "I am most definitely going to whip your bottom, Peter dear. But I'm also going to whip your back—and your shoulders, and your legs too."

"For God's sake, no!"

"Yes, Peter." Her tone was implacable.

He tugged in desperation at his bonds. Perhaps he could get free before she started. He succeeded only in cutting his skin with the twine. His ankles and wrists were immovable. She had done the tying very efficiently. He gave a great sigh of hopelessness and buried his face into the pillow again.

Susan raised the whip slowly and deliberately. She aimed with her eye at the centre of his buttocks. She brought the whip down hard. It gave a little hiss and then a *chuck* as it bit into his flesh.

His head jerked out of the pillow. He gave an agonised shout.

She struck again at the same place.

He screamed.

The scream was like a heady wine to her. She struck again, this time across his shoulder-blades.

His scream changed to a screech. It reverberated through and round the bedroom.

She let her whip-hand fall. "This won't do," she said. "You're making too much noise. We'll have the police on us." She regarded him thoughtfully. She would have tho gag him, but what with? Then she thought of something. Her stockings would make a perfect gag.

She threw the whip on to the bed and lifted her skirt. She took off her stockings quickly. She rolled one of them into a ball. She climbed on to the bed and sat down on his back. "Lift your head, Peter. Open your mouth."

Out of the corner of his eye he had watched her take off her stockings and had wondered, amid the waves of agony that clutched at his body, why she was doing so. Now he understood that he was to be gagged—to be made more helpless than ever. The prospect was so shocking that he felt faint.

He shook his head violently and buried it more deeply into the pillow.

"Oh," she said. "It's like that, is it?" She sat astride his back, thinking. She had him so much at her mercy that she should be able in some way to force the stocking into his mouth. But how? An idea—a thrilling idea—suddenly came to her mind.

She moved off his back and put a hand between his legs. "You like me to squeeze your john-thomas, don't you, my dear? How would you like me to squeeze your balls?" She took hold of the bag of his testicles. "I've heard that his is the worst thing that can be done to a man—but if you're going to be disobedient..." She began to squeeze. She watched intently for his reaction.

It came at once. He lifted his head and said, in a panic-filled voice. "No! Not that! Please!" Even the whip across his back was not so bad as this.

"Are you going to open your mouth, as I told you to do?"

He nodded silently.

She straddled his back again. "Open it, then." She felt a sort of dizzy rapture at the realisation of the power she now had over him. "Come on, open it wide." She reached forward and stuffed the stocking into his mouth. "Hold your head up a moment more." She reached for her other stocking and looped it between his teeth. She pulled it tight and tied it behind his head. "Now we'll be a bit safer," she said judiciously. "It's a pity to have to do it. I *like* to hear you scream like that, but we don't want to have the neighbours and the police arriving, do we?"

She climbed off his back and took up her position beside the bed again. She reached for her whip. She ran its lash through her left hand and, at the same time, moistened her lips with her tongue.

She moved her position a little, and raised the whip. She began to lash with a good deal of force. She lashed quite slowly—a stroke every three seconds.

Each time the whip cut into his flesh, Peter grunted and groaned in agony.

Susan aimed six times at his buttocks. Then she lashed him once across the shoulders and once across the tender flesh a little above the back of his knees. Then she started again on his buttocks.

A fierce, burning ecstasy began to possess her. She lifted her skirt with her free hand. She pushed her hand inside her panties. She stroked and caressed the wet lips of her vagina. She knew that she would have an orgasm very soon. In the midst of her ecstasy she marvelled at her stupidity, as she now saw it, for not having had the courage to do this before. This was giving her the sort of heaven she had so often dreamed about.

It was giving Peter an idea of what hell might be like. During the first thirty or forty lashes he thought he would go out of his mind. Then, slowly, the pain began to be a little less excruciating. He did not know it, but his nerve centres were becoming auto-anaesthetized. Each lash still seared him—particulary those across his back—but they began gradually to be almost bearable. And as the pain became less excruciating, there began to grow, deep down in his loins, a titillating feeling such as he had never before experienced in sex. It advanced and receded, advanced and receded—and soon he began to understand that it advanced immediately after the lash-induced pain gripped him, and it receded during the three-second pause before the whip struck again. It was an intoxicating pleasure, each time it advanced and laid its hands on his genital nerves.

Amid his torment of pain and pleasure, he remembered Susan's words, just after they had come home from the cinema. "It's agony at first, apparently—but then they get a pleasure out of it." It seemed that she had known what she was talking about.

Despite the intoxicating, titillating pleasure, however, her lashes still gave him so much pain that he longed for her to stop. But they went on, relentlessly—lash after lash after lash.

With one part of her brain, Susan knew that she ought to stop. She had given him well over a hundred lashes now. He was covered with blood-filled weals, and she herself was spattered with the drops of blood that now jumped into the air each time her whip descended. But she was in the grip of an impending orgasm and she could not make herself stop. The orgasm had been teetering at its peak for the last thirty lashes or so, and each further lash seemed to give an unearthly caress to her every genital organ. A few more lashes and the orgasm would take her in its teeth...

About fifteen lashes later, it did so. It took her, shook her, ravaged her. And all through the length of it she thrashed on, her eyes closed, her whip falling wherever it would. An ineffable sweetness flooded through her body, a sweetness she had never dreamed could exist in life. It lasted for almost a full minute, and when it finally drained away it left her utterly exhausted and fainting. She dropped the whip to the floor and collapsed forward on to the bed, her face falling into the blood of the lacerated buttocks.

Peter realised it was over. Amid his feeling of relief and release, there was, however, a sense of nostalgia for the intoxicating, titillating, pleasurable sensation that had stopped after the last lash. He lay still, feeling he weight of her head on his bottom, and realising for the first time how fast his heart was beating.

It was a full five minutes before she raised her head. "Are you all right, Peter?" When there was no reply, she had a shock of fear. Then she remembered that he was gagged. She sat up and untied the stocking at the back of his head. She leaned over and took the other one from his mouth. "Are you all right?" she repeated.

"Yes," he said, in a surprisingly vigorous voice. "And I'm very randy. Get these ropes off me, will you? I want to poke you. And you're going to be poked as you've never been poked before."

II

A POTENTIALLY DANGEROUS SITUATION

When dinner was over, the six of them went into the living-room to have coffee. Mr. Blake lit his pipe and quietly studied the four young people. His daughter Marianne, just eighteen years old, was an exceptionally lovely young woman, he thought. Her friend Elisabeth, sitting beside his wife on the sofa, was the same age and almost equally lovely. He sighed and wished he were twenty years younger. It would be very nice to make love to Elisabeth. He looked at his son John, tall and well-built, and looking older than his seventeen years. He suppressed the smile that sprang to his lips. John was gazing at Elisabeth with an obvious yearning. Yes, thought Mr. Blake, he is wishing the same thing. He turned his eyes to Elisabeth's brother Paul, also handsome, well-built and seventeen years old. This time he could not suppress the smile. Paul, fidgeting with some magazines at a side table, was virtually eating Marianne with his eyes.

A potentially dangerous situation, thought Mr. Blake. Four very goodlooking young people in the house for the week-end, and the two boys in an obvious frustration over the two girls. He wondered whether the girls were still virgins. It did not occur to him to wonder whether the boys were still virginal. He had had his own first sexual adventure at the age of fifteen. He assumed that his son, and his son's friend, must by now have broken their celibacy.

He was wrong. John and Paul were still both celibate. Not, of course, because they did not want a sexual adventure, but because of lack of opportunity. Each of them had yearned for the other's sister for over two years now, and each of them would have given a great deal for the opportunity, but that opportunity seemed always to elude them. That afternoon, the four of them had been riding. They had reached a wood, dismounted, tied their horses, and entered the shade of the dense trees. They lay down on the soft loamy earth. But, somehow, it seemed impossible to them both to go any further. Their shyness was an impregnable wall that they dared not climb, though they longed for the paradise that they knew they would find on the other side.

They had no idea how irritated the girls were at this timidity. Elisabeth and Marianne were both hot-blooded young females, and neither was a virgin. They wished they could strip the trousers off these gauche young men, and guide their penises to where they should be put. But their upbringing and innate delicacy prevented it. They too faced a wall of shyness. And so the four of them returned home for dinner in a state of intense frustration.

"What would you like to do?" asked Mrs. Blake of no one in particular. "What about a game of rummy?"

"Oh Mother, not rummy!" said John at once. "Let's play pontoon."

"And lose all your pocket-money." Mrs. Blake

looked doubtfully at her husband, but he, fully agreeing with his son, carefully avoided her eyes.

"Either that," said John, "or win a good deal more."

"I don't approve very much of pontoon," said his mother. "You remember what happened the last time you all played it. The thing got completely out of hand."

John was taking the cards out of a drawer. "We'll fix a limit," he said.

"And mind you stick to it," said Mr. Blake with mock severity.

The six of them played pontoon for an hour or so. John lost all his pocket-money. When he tried to borrow some more from his father, his mother put her foot down and the game broke up. Mr. Blake glanced at the clock and yawned. "Time for bed, perhaps?"

Paul was sharing John's bedroom, Elisabeth Marianne's. The house was of but medium size and an extra single bed had been put into each of the children's rooms in order to permit them to have their friends to stay.

Paul sighed as John shut the door behind him. "Oh God, I'm randy. I thought we were very nearly there this afternoon."

"So did I," said John. "But there was an expression in Elisabeth's eyes that wasn't exactly a green light."

"I've got to have a woman soon—somehow."

"With the money you've just won from me you can go up to town and buy one."

Paul shook his head. "I don't mean a whore. I mean a girl, and preferably your sister."

"And I want yours," said John gloomily. "It's a hell of a situation. And I'm as randy as a ram myself. I suppose we'll have to toss each other off again." He opened his fly and brought out an enormous penis. "Come on, get yours out too."

In their room a few yards away, Marianne and

Elisabeth were discussing their own desires. "It makes me want to scream," said Elisabeth. "Why, why, why are they so damn scared?"

"What makes *me* want to scream," said Marianne, "is that we are so damn scared too. We should do something about it. Take their trousers down, for instance."

Elisabeth chuckled. "Yes, we should. Why don't we, next time?"

Marianne stared at her. "Are you serious?"

Elisabeth stared back, thoughtfully. "I wasn't, actually. But now I think of it, why not? Why shouldn't we? We know that they both want us."

"Our ladylike upbringing!" said Marianne acidly. "Some things are not done."

"To hell with being a lady. I want to have John inside me."

"Yes, I know how you feel. I'm just dying to be ravished by Paul."

There was a silence. Elisabeth picked up the switch which she had thrown on her bed when they returned from their riding. She lashed at her pillow with it, her anger at the situation burning like fire inside her. She wished that the pillow was John's backside. "Marianne," she said suddenly, and threw down the switch.

"Yes?"

"Why *don't* we do something about it?"

"Seriously?"

"Yes, seriously. The whole thing is too silly for words."

Marianne looked at her curiously. "When?"

Elisabeth paused for a second. "Why not now?"

"Good heavens!"

"Why not? Why don't we just go into their bedroom and seduce them? The silly asses simply have to be shown the way. They wouldn't if they came from anywhere near the Mediterranean, but they're English, poor things. Let's go and show them the way. Come on."

Marianne's eyes began to shine. "Yes. Yes, really. Why not?" She gazed at her friend meditatively, touching the idea cautiously, feeling it, testing it and finally, with a flood of excitement, accepting it. "My God, why not? Come on."

"Let's visit the bathroom first."

"Have you got any french-letters? I don't suppose they have."

"Yes, I never travel without them. I don't want a baby yet."

Marianne laughed. "I don't know which of us is the more awful."

Outside the door of John's bedroom they hesitated and looked at each other. Something of their determination had disappeared as they had tip-toed down the passage. "Should we knock?" breathed Elisabeth.

Marianne shook her head. "Let's just burst in and surprise them."

"Suppose the door is locked?"

"John never locks the door."

Elisabeth put her hand to the handle and took a breath. "All right, come on." She turned the handle and opened the door abruptly. She walked quickly into the room. "My God!" she said.

Marianne followed her and quickly shut the door behind her. She stared at the scene in front of them. Her eyes opened very wide. Oho!" she said. "So this is what goes on, is it?" Her voice was cold and angry.

John and Paul were lying on one of the beds. They were naked. They lay flat on their backs, masturbating each other with their fingers.

They looked up at the girls dazedly for some seconds, unable to speak. The scene was like some orgiastic painting.

Elisabeth glared at her brother furiously. "Haven't

you grown out of that yet?" She glanced at John and felt more furious than ever. What a waste of time and strength it was. "You should be whipped, both of you," she said icily.

"I've a very good idea that Daddy *will* whip you," Marianne said to John. "Grown-up though you think you are."

John licked his lips. "You're surely not going to tell him?" He swung his legs off the bed and stood up. He reached for his trousers. His voice showed his fear.

Marianne snatched the trousers away from him. "Just stay like that, while we decide what to do with you." She looked him up and down contemptuously. His penis, which had been mightily erected a moment before, was growing smaller and smaller. She watched it in angry fascination.

Paul got to his feet and then sat down again on the side of the bed. "Why the devil didn't we lock the door?" he muttered.

"Is that all you can say?" demanded his sister. "You're not ashamed of yourself then? Masturbating at your age?" She realised that her voice was rising. She made an effort to control herself. "Why don't you have a woman if you're so sex-starved?"

"That's not so easy as you think."

"Not so easy!" She laughed sarcastically. "If you'd had a spark of manhood in you, you'd've had Marianne in the woods this afternoon." She looked at John. "And you would have had me."

John's eyes opened wide. "I wish I'd known. I've wanted you for as long as I can remember."

"Well, it's a bit late now, isn't it?"

Marianne said suddenly. "They *ought* to be whipped, I agree. Let's do it ourselves."

Elisabeth turned her head slowly. "Let's *whip* them ourselves, you mean?"

"Yes. We could really give them something to remember."

"You mean now? Here?"

"Why not?"

"Your father and mother. Won't they hear?"

"No. Their room is too far away."

John said suddenly. "Now, look!"

"Shut up," said Marianne, "or I'll double the whipping and report you as well."

Elisabeth moistened her lips. "All right," she said softly. "Let's give them something to remember. I'll go and get our switches."

"They've got their own here," said Marianne. "Where are they?" she demanded, looking menacingly at her brother.

"In the wardrobe," he said sulkily.

"Get them."

He went to the wardrobe and took out his switch and Paul's. He handed them to Marianne. "You can't get away with this," he said.

She looked steadily into his eyes. "Don't say that again," she said evenly. "You're going to be whipped by us and you can't do anything about it. Not unless you prefer Mummy and Daddy to know what we caught you doing."

"And that," said Elisabeth to Paul, "goes for you too. You'll be punished now by us, or I'll report the whole thing as soon as we get home."

Paul looked her in the eyes and shook his head. "I don't think you'd do that, Liz. You've never been a sneak."

"I've never been so angry," she replied convincingly. "I mean it. You'll accept a whipping or be reported. Which is it to be?"

He sighed. He looked at John and shrugged his shoulders. "Better grin and bear it, I suppose."

John glanced at the switches in Marianne's hand.

He was silent for a moment. "I suppose so," he said at length.

Marianne was examining the switches. Her heart was beating fast. She suddenly realised that she was looking forward to what she was going to do. It was an exciting thought. "I'm going to enjoy this," she said candidly. "But these are too short and thick. Ours will be better."

"Yes, much better," said Elisabeth. "Longer and swishier. I'll go and get them."

In her bedroom she leaned against the bedpost for a moment. Her heart was pounding, too. Her anger had been gradually evaporating for some moments. It was being replaced by an enticing feeling of excitement. She picked up her switch from the bed where she had thrown it, took Marianne's from the wardrobe, and went quickly back to the others. She locked the door behind her.

The young men looked fearfully at the switches in her hand. They were each nearly a yard long, of leather-covered whalebone. They would give a great deal of pain.

John swallowed some saliva. "How many are you going to give us?"

Elisabeth answered in a quiet, even voice. "If Marianne agrees, we shall whip you for half an hour." She took a deep breath, for she had felt that her voice would begin to tremble if she said any more.

Marianne hid her surprise. She had been thinking in terms of a school-master's twelve of the best. But this was a very good idea. "I fully agree."

John and Paul spoke simultaneously. "But that's impossible, absurd! It's out of the question! Whoever heard of such a thing?" Their tones showed their incredulity. "You must be joking!"

Elisabeth handed one of the switches to Marianne. "You'll accept it without any further argument, or be reported." Her voice trembled a little this time.

Marianne looked at her brother and then at Paul. "Wouldn't it be better," she said slowly, "if I whip your brother and you whip mine."

Elisabeth had had this thought at the back of her mind, but had hesitated to express it. "Yes," she said gratefully. "Much better. Shall we do it together or one after the other?"

"Oh, together," said Marianne breathlessly. "I'm dying to start." She pointed with her switch to Paul's bed. "Lie down there—on your tummy."

Paul felt a chill run through him. He did not like the look in her eyes. He hesitated for a second and then obeyed. He heard Elisabeth say: "And you, John, bend over your bed. I'll thrash you lying down later on."

Marianne said suddenly. "We'd better tie them up, hadn't we?"

"I don't know," said Elisabeth. "They've got to take it, and they know it. They'll have to do as we say."

"Perhaps we'd better tie their ankles though. We don't want them squirming about."

"This is all going too far," said John. "I don't know what's got into you both."

There was a sound of a switch hissing through the air.

"Ouch!" he exclaimed as it lashed across his buttocks.

Elisabeth moistened her lips. The lash had given her a surprising stab of pleasure in her loins. "We told you not to argue," she said.

"Ties," said Marianne. "Those would do wonderfully for their ankles." She turned to John. "Go and get two old ties."

"I haven't any old ties," he said sulkily.

Elisabeth's switch struck his buttocks again. He went to a chest of drawers and rummaged among his ties. He pulled two out. He gave one to his sister and returned to Elisabeth. He handed her the other tie and bent over the bed again.

Elisabeth knelt beside him. "Close your feet together." She tied the tie tightly round his ankles. She stood up. "Now," she said, and moistened her lips again. "Here comes the first part. But don't make any noise or I'll gag you too. And that wouldn't be pleasant, would it?"

"I don't see that it would make much difference."

She put a hand to his penis. It erected almost at once. He looked at her in amazement.

"You see," she said softly. "After I've given you twenty or so, I might let you kiss me. And you couldn't do that if you were gagged, could you?" She fondled his penis and then released it. She stepped back. "So here they come."

Marianne had watched the fondling of her brother's penis. She now looked down at Paul's naked back. She put a hand down and stroked his buttocks. They quivered under her cool fingers. She put her hand between his legs and under his body. She felt for his penis. It grew in her hand. She said: "You heard what Elisabeth said to my brother. The same thing can happen to you, if you're very good and obedient." She stood up. "And now comes *your* first part." She raised her switch and brought it down across the centre of his buttocks. They gave a sharp quiver as the switch cut into them. She saw Elisabeth, out of the corner of her eye, beginning her own whipping.

Neither of the young men made a sound. Without analysing it, they both instinctively felt that it would be shameful to let the girls hear them protest and complain. They gritted their teeth and suffered the pain silently.

There was a good deal of pain, although neither Marianne nor Elisabeth were using anything like their whole strength. To whip young men across their naked bottoms was so much of a novelty that a trace of shyness remained in the midst of their pleasure and enjoyment. Gradually, however, the shyness wore away and both the girls began to hit harder.

When she had delivered about twenty strokes, Marianne sat heavily down on the side of the bed, panting with breathless excitement. She put a hand to Paul's bottom and ran her fingers lightly across his weals. He flinched.

"How did you like that?" she said softly. "That's what you get for being a bad boy."

He made no reply. His teeth were still gritted with the pain that continued to course through him.

"You behaved like a naughty little boy," she went on. "And naughty little boys must be whipped. Soundly whipped." She put her hand between his legs again. His penis was soft and small, but it began to erect at once under her touch. She caressed it for a moment or two. Then she removed her hand and stood up. "They must be very soundly whipped, so that they shall not do the same thing again." She raised her switch and continued with the thrashing. Her heart was beating fast, her breath coming in short gasps. She was experiencing a feeling of wild, burning sexual hunger. She realised that she would not be able to continue whipping him for the full half-hour. She would have to have him soon, or faint. But she would give him another twenty very hard lashes at least. She called on all her strength.

Elisabeth had also stopped for a breather. "You can stand up, if you like," she said to John, as she too flopped on to the side of the bed. She sat with her head lowered, listening to the thud of her heart.

John stood upright and massaged his buttocks with is hands. "You're a devil," he said quietly. "Either a devil or a sadist."

She raised her head. "Perhaps I *am* a sadist," she said reflectively. "At any rate, I'm enjoying this very much indeed. Is it very bad?"

"Yes," he said shortly.

"I'm glad," she answered simply. "But you asked for it, you know."

He looked at her and felt the ache of longing once more. His buttocks were on fire, but he desired her very strongly. He reached down and took one of her hands. He guided it to his penis. "Will you do that again, please?" Now that she had whipped him, he no longer had any shyness. He wondered at his own, and Paul's, stupidity. They had wasted a lot of time.

She squeezed his penis. "I'll do something better," she said. "Come a little nearer." She moved her position so that she was sitting squarely on the edge of the bed. When he moved closely in front of her, she lowered her head and put her lips to his penis.

He stiffened as much with surprise as with pleasure. He felt her lips on the central nerve of the penis. Then he felt her warm moist tongue running up and down it. And then he felt the whole of the penis being engulfed by her mouth. He stretched back his shoulders as though he were leaning against a soft wall of pure ecstasy. He moaned slightly. He put his hands down to her chest, slipped his fingers inside her dress and took hold of her nipples lightly.

Elisabeth gave a quiver of delight at his touch. She sucked his penis and bit it lightly and caressed it with her tongue for a few more moments. Then she slowly withdrew it from her mouth.

He gave a great sigh. "Oh God!" he murmured. "Oh God!"

She smiled up at him. "Nice?"

"Oh God! I didn't imagine you'd ever do that."

"No, I don't suppose you did."

"You're not a virgin, are you?" It seemed impossible that a virgin could do such a thing so unembarrassedly.

"No, John. I'm not a virgin."

"How many times? I mean——"

"I know what you mean. Once."

"I'll bet he wasn't an Englishman."

She laughed merrily. "You're quite astute, aren't you? No, he wasn't an Englishman. And, of course, he taught me to do that. Otherwise I don't suppose I'd ever have learned."

He gazed at her with hungry, burning eyes. "Do it again, please."

She shook her head and stood up. "Not now. Later perhaps. A little more whipping now. Lie down this time. On your tummy."

He opened his mouth to protest, but thought better of it. He shrugged his shoulders. He lay down on the bed and put his face into the pillow. He determined to put his thoughts and concentration on what they would do together when the whipping was finally finished. In that way he might ignore some of the pain.

He realised how wrong he was as the switch cut across his buttocks again...

Marianne was counting: "...eighteen ...nineteen ...twenty." She dropped the switch and fell forward with. all her length over Paul's body. She pressed her stomach against his buttocks, the weals of which were now bleeding slightly. She realised she would spoil her dress but she was in too advanced a state of sexual yearning to care. "The half-hour is not up by any means," she whispered in his ear. "But I can't go on. I want to make love. Come on, turn over." She moved herself off his body, turned on her back, and lay flat beside him.

Painfully he began to raise himself.

"Don't touch the bed with your bottom," she said quickly. "It's covered with blood. You'd better get something to lie on. But be quick."

"Will you untie my feet," he said. "I can't manage to get off the bed like this. I shall touch everything."

"Oh yes, I forgot your feet." She sat up and untied the tie around his ankles. She flopped back and closed her eyes. "Be quick," she repeated.

Paul climbed off the bed and stood irresolutely, wondering what he could lie on.

"Two or three handkerchiefs," she said, without opening her eyes. "One on top of the other."
"Yes," he said. "Of course."
When he returned to the bed, her eyes were still closed. One hand, however, was held up. In it was a rolled-up french-letter. "Put this on," she murmured. "I don't want a baby yet."
He looked at her in surprise. He had not considered the necessity of a french-letter. He was glad her eyes were shut. He felt very foolish. He looked down at his penis. It was standing mightily against his stomach. He rolled the letter over it and lay down beside her on the bed. He took her in his arms and kissed her. He wondered how long he ought to go on doing this before he could put the throbbing penis where it wanted to go.
She flung her arms round his neck, hugged him hard, returned his kiss passionately, and then disengaged herself gently. "Let's not waste time," she said softly.
He lifted her skirt and reached for her panties. He pulled them down. "They're wet," he said, in surprise.
"Of course they're wet!"
"Good Lord!"
"Yes," she said dreamily. "It was heaven, whipping you. And I'm going to do it again."
"Now that I know I can do this with you, you won't have the excuse."
She felt the hard penis sliding inside her. She heard Elisabeth say: "That's enough for the time being, at any rate. Turn over and make love to me now." The penis slid further and further inside her. She moaned with pleasure. She said: "Maybe I won't have *that* excuse for whipping you, but I'll certainly find another."

III

A LITTLE MUSIC WHILE YOU WORK

O'Brian stood in the doorway of his cell, waiting for the whistles that would instruct him and the other convicts on this landing that it was their turn to go to the foul-smelling water-closet to empty the slops that they had accumulated during the previous evening and night. He trembled as he waited.

The warders in the prison rarely gave their orders by voice. Whenever they could, they preferred to put their whistles to their lips, blow them loud and screechingly, and let the prisoners guess what they were being ordered to do. It was not, of course, difficult for them to guess this because the routine of the prison was very regular, and they performed all its motions like automata. The thing that was beginning to infuriate O'Brian again, however, was that when one warder put his whistle to his lips and blew it, all other warders in his vicinity did the same thing, as though they wanted to support with their own authority the order, great or small, that the original whistler was giving.

So O'Brian stood, trembling, with his fists clenched, waiting.

When the whistle came, taken up at once by half a dozen others, he flinched as though he had been struck. Shaking with impotent anger, he made his way along the landing with his poe, emptied his slops, returned to his cell, put the poe in its position, and returned to the doorway of the cell, waiting for the whistles that would this time signal the march to work.

Later, in the gloom of one of the prison workshops, he sat sewing coal-bags. He tried to let his mind go blank. If there had to be whistles he was foolish to allow them to drive him to the edge of a nervous collapse. He ought by now to have become accustomed to them. He must try to control his nerves. There was not so much longer to go. Only two months and one week. And, perhaps, in one week's time, there might be a chance of his being put into an outside working-party.

It was the practice, in that prison in the north of England, to restrict the privilege of working outside the workshops to those of the prisoners who had no more than two months of their sentences to serve. It was thought that they would be less tempted to try to escape than those who had a longer time to serve. No working-parties ever went outside the prison walls, but nevertheless escape would have been slightly less difficult than from the interior work-shops. So great, however, was the desire of the prisoners to achieve the privilege of joining one of the groups that worked in the potato-field, or swept the yards and roads of the prison, or repaired and painted the exterior woodwork, or laboured on any of the multifarious outside-jobs required by an efficient administration, that no one ever attempted to escape. It was a privilege to be prized, not jeopardised.

A greater privilege, of course, was that of being appointed librarian. True, one did not work outside, but one had the illusion of some freedom of movement. The greatest privilege of all, however, was that of becoming the servant of the Chief Warder. One left one's cell in the morning and returned to it at night. In the meantime, one worked at congenial housekeeping tasks, and had one's midday meal in the kitchen of the house, eating the same food as the Chief Warder and his daughter ate in their dining-room. The fact that the daughter was a very lovely girl of about twenty-six was regarded by the lucky appointee as an extra bonus sent straight from heaven.

O'Brian wondered whether he had any chance at all of becoming the new librarian. The present librarian had only another three weeks to serve. He shook his head. It was hoping for too much. There were too many others who could be appointed to the job. His only hope was that he had had a university education, and was therefore a more logical choice than most of the others. But he had no faith in his luck any longer.

The job of servant in the Chief Warder's house would be free soon, too. In about ten days. What price his chances there? He grinned at his thought. It was like asking for the moon. No, let him only get himself on the potato-field party, or something else like it, and he would be very happy. He would at least get out of this constantly gloomy light, out of these claustropobia-producing walls, away from the stench of unwashed bodies, and away—for some hours at any rate—from these bloody whistles.

He winced as a whistle blew again at that moment. Without looking up from his work, he listened to the bellow of the warder. Shouting at the top of his voice at a man who was sitting no further than six feet away from him: "You there, Andrews! Just let me see you talking again and you'll have a week of bread and water." As though to put an emphatic full-stop to what the warder had bellowed, the whistle blew again.

O'Brian sighed. He forced his mind to become as blank as possible.

A little more than a week later, Mary, the daughter of the Chief Warder, looked at her father over the breakfast table. "Jackinson will be getting out in a day or so, won't he? And we'll be needing another servant?"

The Chief Warder grunted, without looking up from his newspaper.

Mary took the grunt to mean assent. "Have you picked anybody to take his place?"

"Not yet."

"When you do, Daddy, will you please pick somebody a little younger than Jackinson. Somebody with a little intelligence too. And nice-looking, if possible."

He glanced up at her. "What's wrong with Jackinson? He's done his work well enough, hasn't he?"

She shrugged. "He's all right, I suppose. Although it took a long time to train him to wash dishes properly. He's such a wizened little squirt, though."

He looked at her blankly. "What do you want, my dear? A servant or a boy-friend?" He regretted his words as he saw the frown come to her face. He said quickly, with a forced smile: "I'm sorry. I didn't mean that." He knew very well that he had meant it, but he dreaded a quarrel. She might leave him and take up that job in the London beauty-parlour that she had been offered. And he would be dreadfully lonely again. Since his wife died, five years ago, he had come to depend very much on the company of his daughter. He knew she hated her secluded life in the prison grounds with nobody to talk to (the wives and daughters of the other prison-officers all lived outside the walls) and with no town of any interest within forty miles. She had left him once to take a job in that town, but, after three months of loneliness, he had begged her to give up the job and come home to him. If she wanted their servant to be young, intelligent and nice-looking—well, he had better find her what she wanted. And he had better close his mind to the suspicions that occasionally came to him. Perhaps she did flirt a bit with whoever was their servant of the moment. Perhaps she went a shade and daughters of the other prison-officers all lived further than flirting. If so, it was her own business. She was free, white and over twenty-one. Let her please herself what she did—so long as she did not leave him alone in an empty house again.

It was because of these suspicions that he had, two months ago, appointed Jackinson as the servant of his household. The two previous ones had been young and presentable—perhaps too presentable, he thought. So he had picked Jackinson who, as Mary said, was a wizened little squirt witout the least possibility of being found presentable. This time, though, he had better fall in with her wishes. He determined to look at his lists when he reached his office, to see which prisoners were coming up for release in the next two months.

He looked at her thoughtfully. "I'll do my best."

"Thank you," she replied coldly, without looking at him. "I'm glad you see the point. You don't have to be at home all day in the company of a little cockney gnome, as ugly as sin. I do—and I hate ugliness, of any sort whatsoever."

"All right, dear," he repeated. "I'll do my best."

In the coal-bag workshop a whistle shrilled.

"O'Brian!" bellowed a warder. "Forward for the Chief Warder. Look sharp!"

O'Brian stood up. He felt suddenly weak from the force of his hope. Perhaps this was his transfer to an outside working-party. A summons from the Chief Warder could surely be for no other reason. To the best of his knowledge, he had done nothing wrong recently. He walked towards the warder.'

"Get a move on," said the warder curtly. "Haven't got all day."

He preceded the warder to the door of the workshop. It was unlocked. He passed through it and was handed over to another warder on the other side. The door was locked behind him.

Five minutes later, after passing through five more doors and being handed over to five different warders, he found himself in the Chief Warder's office. He stood rigidly at attention and waited.

The Chief Warder looked at him searchingly. This, one would certainly please his daughter. Even in the shapeless prison clothes he looked presentable, even handsome. He was also tall, slim and strong-looking. Yes, he would do very well.

Closing his mind firmly against his nagging suspicions, the Chief Warder said: "You're due to get out in a couple of months. So you qualify for some outside job or other. Do you want one?"

"With all my heart, sir," said O'Brian quietly. "Yes please."

The Chief Warder glanced at him. His educated accent was unusual in that prison. "All right. You can go and do the skivvy-work in my house."

O'Brian looked at him speechlessly. The most highly-prized job of all, the one job he had not dared even to dream about, was being offered to him. He swallowed and found his voice. "Thank you very much, sir," he stammered.

"You'll start on Thursday. All right, dismissed."

The escorting warder bellowed in O'Brian's ear: "About turn! March! Look sharp! Haven't got all day!"

On Thursday morning, after his breakfast of a ladleful of watery porridge, a hunk of bread and a diminutive cube of margarine, washed down with a mug of stewed and tepid tea, O'Brian waited with tingling nerves for the summons to his new job. Today, for the first time in over a year, he would not have to sit for interminable hours in the gloom and stench of the coal-bag workshop. He would work in a house, in a human atmosphere, on congenial tasks. His mistress would be the daughter of the Chief Warder, a girl he had once seen at one of the very rare concerts that were given in the prison. At that concert he had gazed at her all the time, for she was a very lovely girl and it was a long time since he had set his eyes on any sort of woman. The thought that he was to work for her now was part of the cause of his tingling nerves.

His cell-door was unlocked. "Ready, O'Brian?" said a warder who was unfamiliar to him. He spoke in a kinder tone of voice than the warders to whom O'Brian was accustomed. Life seemed a good deal better today than he could have hoped for. "You're a lucky fellow," the warder went on. "I suppose you realise that, don't you?"

"I do indeed," said O'Brian fervently.

"You'd better watch your step. You'll be all right till you get out, if you watch your step. But if you put a foot wrong you'll be back stitching coal-bags. Remember that."

"I'll remember it," said O'Brian, feeling that he would be prepared to work like a slave, like ten slaves, rather than return to the coal-bags. "Is she easy to work for? Do you know?"

The warder shook his head. "She's a bit particular, from what I hear. But if you watch your step, you'll be all right."

"What's her name?" O'Brian suddenly realised that he did not know, had never heard, the name of the Chief Warder.

"Miss Langley," said the other. "Mary Langley." He gave a sardonic laugh. "I doubt that you'll be calling her Mary. Just remember your place and call her Miss Langley, or madam or miss. And watch your step. Come on now. I've got to deliver you. And I'll come and get you back this evening."

As O'Brian followed him along the landing, down the black iron stairs, through seemingly innumerable doors, each one of which was unlocked and relocked behind them, he reflected that the rather nice warder who was his escort had warned him no fewer than four times to watch his step. Did it perhaps mean that there was some snag to the job after all? Was Mary Langley a difficult person to work for? He would soon find out. And he would certainly watch his step. On no account would he be sent back to the coal-bags. He was fully decided upon that point.

Mary opened the front door and said good morning briefly to the warder. She looked at O'Brian appreciatively. Her father had chosen well, she thought. This one was a great improvement on Jackinson. It would be stimulating to have him working for her.

She stood aside. "Come in," she said. She nodded her dismissal of the warder. When O'Brian had stepped over the threshold she closed the door and said: "Go into the living-room first." She pointed to a door.

It was a small room and not very luxuriously or expensively furnished. Most of the furniture belonged, in fact, to the prison administration. This did not spend a large amount of money upon the comfort of its officers, even of its Chief Warders. To O'Brian, however, accustomed as he had been for a year to a bare and soulless cell, the room was a paradise of sheer luxury. He had almost forgotten what curtains and cushions and carpets looked like. He stood in the middle of the floor, gazing round him with considerable pleasure.

Mary sat in an armchair, lit a cigarette, crossed her legs and studied him.

"First, what is your name?" she asked crisply.

"O'Brian, Miss Langley," he replied, after a second's pause. The pause had been due to his doubt as to whether to call her miss or madam or by her name.

She nodded. The voice of a gentleman, too. Her father had chosen very well indeed. "How long have you been in?"

"A little over a year."

"What are you in for?"

He was glad she had asked that. He was not, after all, a thief or a criminal of the usual sort. For the sake of his self-esteem he was glad that he had the opportunity of getting that clear to her. If she had been less good-looking, he probably wouldn't have minded so much. As it was, the matter assumed an illogical importance for him. "I killed someone in a car accident," he said quietly. "I'm in for manslaughter."

"And of course it was not your fault." They always said it was not fair that they should be in prison. They were either innocent or the victims of a judge's hostility or something or other. They were never guilty.

He surprised her. "Yes, it was my fault. I admitted it in court. That's why I got a relatively light sentence."

She raised her eyes. "I see. Well, that's very honest of you." She regarded him thoughtfully. "Are you married?"

He shook his head, wondering why she should be interested. "No, Miss Langley."

She stubbed out her cigarette. "Well, you won't find the work hard," she said, in a business-like tone of voice. "If you do it well, there's no reason why you shouldn't keep it till you get out. Don't forget that you answer to me, although you are theoretically my father's servant. If you please me, you'll find I can be quite rewarding."

You are already very rewarding, he was thinking to himself, gazing at her as she spoke. You are like somebody from another world. You are quite incredibly lovely, with your long shapely legs and your tiny waist and those breasts. He caught his breath as he imagined himself stroking them. He pulled himself angrily together. That sort of thought might lead him straight back to the coal-bags.

"Do you smoke?" she was asking.

"Yes," he said. "I smoke my ration."

She reached over to a side table and picked up an unopened packet of cigarettes. "Catch," she said, and tossed it to him. "If you want to smoke here, you can. You'll find matches in the kitchen."

He looked at the packet in his hands with something like awe. The twenty cigarettes represented a whole month's ration. He said, with an effort to keep his voice even: "Thank you very much indeed, Miss Langley."

"And another thing," she said casually. "You look the sort of man who would like more baths than you get in prison. There's plenty of hot water in this house. If you want a bath, just take it. But be sure to take it before my father gets home. That is punctually at two minutes past one and two minutes past six."

He looked at her speechlessly. "Do you mean *every* day, Miss Langley?"

"Yes, if you want. There's always plenty of hot water."

He swallowed. "Thank you very much. I—I hope I shall be able to satisfy you with my work. I'll do my best. You are very kind indeed."

She smiled, as though at some secret thought. "I wonder whether you'll go on thinking so. I shall be a very demanding person to work for. You may be surprised." She stood up abruptly. "Come on. I'll show you what you have to do."

The next three days were something like heaven for O'Brian. The work was pleasant—even the scrubbing of floors was congenial after the coal-bag workshop, he ate well at noon, he was able to smoke when he wanted, and he had a hot bath every morning as soon as he arrived.

It was on the fourth morning, after he had finished his bath and was preparing to wash up the dishes of the family's breakfast and previous evening's supper, that Mary Langley came into the kitchen with a cane in her hand. He looked at it in surprise as he nodded his head respectfully to her, and a sudden chill went through him. He looked into her eyes and then glanced at the cane again. He drew a long, slow breath.

"Yes," she said quietly. "You've guessed correctly."

"Why?" he asked, though he was sure he knew the answer.

"It gives me pleasure."

He nodded his head. "There was bound to be a snag. Everything was too good to be true."

"It won't be too bad," she said, swishing the cane up and down. "Just a little music while you work. Today with this, tomorrow with a whip, the next day with something else. I've got a lot of instruments that make very nice music." She looked a him narrowly. "Unless you'd prefer to go back to your coal-bag sewing."

He shook his head at once. "No. I don't want that."

She swished the cane again. "So you'll take this." It was a statement, not a question.

He shrugged his shoulders. "It seems that I must."

"Take your trousers down then." Her tone was brisk but not unfriendly. "Let's see how tough you are." She went to the window and pulled the gingham curtains across.

He fumbled with the buttons of his trousers. He could hardly believe that he was going to be beaten by her. It was quite obvious, of course, but events had moved so fast that he wondered for an instant whether he could be dreaming.

"Come on, come on!" she said. "Don't take all day. Get your trousers down."

He undid his buttons and let the trousers fall to his ankles. "It's a long time since this happened to me," he said, with forced lightness.

"Where was the last time?"

"At school."

"Where were you?"

He mentioned the name of a famous public school.

"I see," she said. "You're quite an aristocrat, indeed. It'll be even more of a pleasure to thrash you. And you must have had a lot of experience of being caned there. That sort of school goes in for caning, doesn't it?"

"But not," he said, "with one's trousers down."

She laughed. "Perhaps tomorrow you'll have more than your trousers down. You have quite a lot of things in store for you. Come on now. Push your pants down too."

He did as she said.

"Now bend over there." She pointed with the cane at the kitchen table. "Put your stomach flat on the top and stretch your hands over the other side."

He found that he was too tall. His stomach would not reach down to the top of the table. He opened his legs and reduced his height. His stomach now lay flat on the cold plastic-covered surface.

"I'm going to give you ten to begin with," she said, moving herself within the correct distance for aiming. "Don't move. Don't get up. Just be a man and take them." She reached out her free hand and lifted his shirt-tail up over his shoulders. "If you move or get up, I'll really make you wish you hadn't. Just lie there and take them." She raised her cane-arm and brought it down across his naked buttocks with considerable force.

Involuntarily, he uttered a cry and jerked himself upright.

"You've moved," she said grimly. "I told you not to. So you'll have five more as punishment. Get down again. If you move once more I'll thrash you so much that you'll wish you'd never been born."

As the cane struck him again O'Brian gritted his teeth and made no movement. The pain was dreadful, and continued to be dreadful as stroke after stroke cut into his flesh. Upon the tenth or eleventh stroke—he was not sure, for he had lost count in his agony—he felt an almost uncontrollable wave of anger take possession of him. Why, he asked himself savagely, was he submitting to this? Why should he not stand up and take the cane from her, break it into pieces, and go back to his coal-bags? But the thought of the coal-bag workshop with its gloom and stench of unwashed bodies kept him, despite his fury, lying supinely across the table until she had struck him fifteen times.

She drew a breath jerkily. Her pulse was racing. "You can dress yourself now," she said tremulously. "And get back to your work." She went to the sink, turned on a tap, and held the cane under the flow of water. The blood that was on it quickly disappeared. She turned and went to the door. On a side table she saw the packet of cigarettes that she had given him on his first day. She opened it. There were two cigarettes left. "I'll bring you another packet," she said. "You've earned it."

There was, of course, no mirror in O'Brian's cell. When he returned to it and had been locked up for the night, he examined his weals with his fingertips.

The blood had dried but he was surprised at the amount that must have been brought. He poured some water into his hand-bowl and carefully washed his buttocks. He wondered suddenly why he had not done it earlier, in the house in which there was an abundance of hot water. He grinned ruefully to himself as he realised why. He had gone through the rest of the day very carefully and very quietly, determinedly avoiding bringing any attention to himself. He had not been at all sure that Mary Langley would not come back with the cane again. Apart, however, from bringing him another packet of twenty cigarettes and saying "That was nice music, wasn't it?", she had treated him in the same way as she had done in his first three days, and made no reference to what had happened in the morning.

He found it was impossible to sit down for his supper. He wandered around his cell, munching his bread and margarine, and wondering what the next day had in store for him. If it was no worse than today, he could stand it—and would gladly stand it rather than return to the workshop. But she had spoken of a whip. And other instruments, as she had called them. Today's caning was probably only a preliminary. Things might get a good deal worse.

He thought again of the pain of the morning. It had been dreadful at the time, of course, but afterwards—afterwards there had been a certain something that was not unpleasurable. What on earth was it? Pleasure? No, of course not. What pleasure could there be in being thrashed, even if the thrasher was an exceptionally lovely girl? None at all. And yet there had been something. A sort of stimulation, a titillation? Yes, something like that. But why? How?

It came to his mind, suddenly and forcefully, that the "why" and the "how" were answered by the fact that the thrasher was indeed such an exceptionally lovely creature. The stimulation, the titillation, which he had felt, came from the fact that he had been subjected and thrashed by this creature.

Was he then a masochist? He immediately rejected the thought.

He frowned in sudden concentration. There had been a book by an Austrian psychologist. What was his name? Heksel? Yes, something like that. He had claimed that every living man and woman was potentially a masochist, if not a sadist. Good heavens! Was he right, after all?

O'Brian undressed and lay down, on his stomach, on his bed. He wondered, fearfully, what the next day had in store for him. Whatever it was, he told himself determinedly, it would be better than returning to the coal-bags.

He drifted into a half-sleep. When he awoke for a few moments to full consciousness, he realised, to his great surprise, that he had been dreaming about Mary Langley. She had had a long, snaky whip in her hands. He was tied over the kitchen table, stark naked. The whipping was terrible. But he had not minded it in the least. And when it was over, he had put her on the floor, ripped her panties down to her knees, and shown her who was really the master.

After his bath the next day, which he had in a state of alternating depression and anticipation, he went to the kitchen and waited for her to come.

He had filled the sink and sprinkled detergent into the water when he heard the door open. There was a swishing sound, as of a taffeta dress or a rubbberised mackintosh, and the door clicked shut again.

He turned his head, and caught his breath.

She stood just inside the kitchen, one hand still on the handle of the door, the other hand holding a whip with a handle of something that looked like ivory. She had changed her clothes. When she let him into the house, she had been wearing a simple blue linen frock.

Now she was dressed in a floor-length robe of some jet-black shimmery silky material that seemed ripplingly alive even as she stood motionless before him. It was tied at her waist with a long sash. It fell open slightly below her knees, revealing a foot that wore a shoe with a very high stiletto heel. He noticed that the leg was bare.

He gazed at her, feeling weak. He had never, he thought, seen so lovely a woman. She was quite unbelievably desirable.

He saw the whip in her hand. She was going to thrash him again, and that was that. But it would be she, this lovely creature, who would do the thrashing, would give the pain. It occurred to him that he did not fear the pain very much. She did not have unlimited strength, after all. He ought to be able to stand whatever she could give. He felt his depression becoming again a feeling of something like excited anticipation.

"My God!" he said quietly.

She smiled. "My God, what?"

"You are very lovely. I've never seen anyone so lovely."

She held up the whip. "This is lovely too, isn't it?" Her robe rustled mysteriousy as she moved her arm.

He shook his head. "I don't think I can agree with that."

She moved, with a deep swoosh of the robe, into the centre of the room. "I'll make you admit it," she said ominously. "Now, would you like to kiss me?"

"Good God!" he said incredulously. "Do you mean it?"

"Why not?" She moved her shoulders as though straining her breasts against the material of her robe. "Why shouldn't you have a bit of pleasure too?"

He grabbed a towel, wiped his hands dry and moved to her. He took her in his arms and put his lips to hers. Hungrily, he forced his tongue between her teeth. His senses swimming after the long months of sexual abstinence, he sucked her tongue into his mouth. She responded passionately. He slipped a hand inside her robe and felt for her breasts. He found that she was quite naked beneath the robe. She answered his gesture by lowering a hand to his flies, unfastening two or three buttons, and seizing his penis.

He groaned, and squeezed her hard against his body.

After a few moments, she pushed him away, breathlessly. "Enough of that for the time being. Although I must say you do it very nicely." She raised the whip to his lips. "Kiss that, too."

His eyes on hers, he obeyed her. When he had kissed the instrument, he said: "You said 'For the time being.' Are you going to let me do it again?" He put his penis-tip back inside his trousers. "And are you going to hold this again?"

She drew the whip through her fingers. "You're talking too much. Just do as I say, and don't ask so many questions."

He nodded his head penitently. "What do you want me to do?"

"First of all, strip." She moved to the curtains and drew them across.

"You mean *all* my clothes?"

"Yes, all of them."

He did not hesitate. He pulled off his clothes quickly and stood before her stark naked. "What happens, though, if somebody comes?" he said curiously.

"Nobody will come." Her tone was definite. It was obvious that she knew beyond doubt that they would not be interrupted.

"But suppose your father were to come back for something," he persisted, wondering what purpose he thought he was serving by the persistence. "Suppose he forgot something when he left this morning and came back to get it. What then?"

She smiled into his eyes. It was a smile compounded of both cruelty and hunger. She flickered her gaze over his muscular body again. Oh yes, she thought, with deliberate and conscious cruelty: it is going to be heaven to flog this body. She looked at his penis, still stiff with the memory of the touch of her fingers. And it is going to be heaven, she thought, to use that later for its proper purpose. "You are very frightened, aren't you? You are wishing that there *could* be a chance of my father coming back for something, aren't you? But there is not the slightest chance of that. Not the slightest. So get it out of your head."

His eyes on the whip, he nodded. He did not speak.

"Would you like to know why there's not the slightest chance?"

He still did not speak. He continued to gaze at the instrument that was going to hurt him. He did indeed feel very frightened. His earlier feeling of excited anticipation had utterly vanished.

"He has gone to London," she said. "He won't be back till late tonight."

He sighed. "Oh," was all that he could say.

"And nobody else will come," she said. "So just make up your mind that you're absolutely at my mercy, and take what is coming to you." She looked suddenly at him with her eyebrows raised in pretended enquiry. "Unless you'd prefer to go back to the coal-bag shop? Is that it, perhaps?"

"No," he said, swallowing some saliva that had gathered in his mouth. "No, I'll take what is coming."

She had had no doubt of it but the dejection of his voice made her suddenly sorry for him. "Come here," she said softly. "Come and kiss me again."

His heart gave a leap. He moved forward at once and took her in his arms. Her robe felt delightfully cold against his naked flesh. He felt for her nipples as her hands seized his penis once again. His heart began to pound heavily. His feeling of excited anticipation returned with a rush. All right, he told himself, so she's going to whip you a bit. So what! You just grin and bear it!

After a few moments she disengaged herself gently. "Come on," she said, with something like a caress in her voice. "You have to have a whipping first. This sort of thing comes afterwards."

Aha ! he thought triumphantly. That's all I wanted to know. Now I can grin and bear it more easily.

"Move the table to one side," she ordered. "I want the middle of the floor free."

She stood aside as he put the table against the wall. Her robe made its usual mysterious rustling sound.

He glanced up at her. "May I please ask something?"

"I don't know whether I shall answer," she said. "But you can ask."

"What *is* the material of that robe you're wearing?"

She laughed. She put a hand to the front of the robe, just above her knees, and drew it aside. She turned the material to show him its inside. He saw her beautiful naked legs beneath it as she did so. "It's rubberised silk," she said. "Silk on the outside and rubber on the inside—next to my body."

"So that's why it rustles so much."

She let the front fall back into place. "Do you like it?"

"Very much indeed. It looks extremely fetching. And it smells nice."

"That's the mixture of the rubber with the perfume I use."

"But why rubber?" he said curiously. "Silk I can understand. But rubber?"

She moved her position abruptly. The conversation was dragging on too long. "I like the feeling of it," she said shortly. "Now, come on."

He was looking at her reflectively. "Yes," he said slowly, as though speaking more to himself than to her. "I can see it now. Smooth rubber. There's nothing smoother, is there? And cool, too. Smooth coolness against the skin. Yes."

She lifted her whip ominously. "Come on," she repeated. "You talk too much." She pointed to the kitchen dresser. "In the drawer there, you'll find some rope and some handcuffs. Bring them here."

The handcuffs were of shining stainless steel. The rope was about a yard long and like a thin pencil in thickness. He put them into her hand. "So you're going to tie me up?"

"Oh yes," she said lightly. "It wasn't necessary yesterday, but you'll have to be made helpless today." She threw the whip on to the table.

He frowned. "The threat of going back to the coal-bag shop surely makes me helpless enough." The handcuffs, in this situation, were very frightening.

"Perhaps it does, and then again, perhaps it doesn't." She was unlocking the handcuffs. "I like to make sure. Now, come on, hold out your wrists." She clicked the manacles tightly shut. "It's useful being a prison-officer's daughter, isn't it? Where would I ever find any handcuffs if I weren't?"

He did not think she really wanted him to reply to that question.

"And now," she went on, making a small loop in the centre of the rope. "Open your legs wide."

"*Open* them!" he exclaimed in great surprise. "Surely you mean close them?"

"I do not," she said patiently. "I said open them and I mean open them."

He obeyed her, wondering what on earth she was going to do. To his intense surprise he saw her bring the loop of rope near to his genitals. Then he felt her take hold of his testicle-bag and slip the loop over it. Christ!" he breathed, moving his manacled hands to one side so that he could see as well as feel what she was doing. "What are you going to do?"

She glanced up at him. Her eyes were dancing with

excitement. "I'm going to make you properly helpless. That's what I'm going to do—among other things." She pulled the loop tight as though the testicle bag were a balloon that had been blown up and was now being tied around its neck with string.

As her fingers moved lightly over his tecticle-bag, his penis re-erected violently. The sensation was sweet, particularly as she drew the loop tighter than ever and made a knot. When the knot was fast, she drew the lengths of rope all the way free so that they hung down the front of his legs. "This knob of yours," she said, giving the penis a slap, "is a nuisance. It's in the way. Why don't you make it go soft?" She slapped it again harder. Then, feeling the exhilaration of sadistic pleasure flood through her, she slapped it again and again and again, harder each time. She looked up at him with shining eyes. "Do as I tell you. Make it go soft!"

With each slap, painful though they were, his penis seemed to grow ever larger and harder. He began to enjoy the pain a little.

She took hold of the dangling ends of rope. She pulled, quite gently. After the ferocity of her slaps it was a wonder to him that she could still retain such control over herself. Gentle though her pull was, however, it caused him a good deal of pain, but, once more, it was pain that was in some curious and indescribable manner sweet and rather exciting. "I'll castrate you," she said, "if you're not careful." She gave another pull, aimed a last stinging slap at the penis, and stepped back from him. "Now kneel down," she said breathlessly. She pointed to the middle of the floor. "There. Kneel down on your knees. Close your feet together now. Yes, that's right."

He obeyed her, again wondering dazedly what was going to happen now.

"Now sit back on your ankles," she ordered. "Like the Japanese do." She watched him approvingly as he did as she commanded. "Yes, you're quite intelligent, aren't you? Most men don't understand so quickly."

"But what are you going to do?" he said, looking up at her in puzzlement.

She chuckled. "You haven't figured that out yet, though! You'll soon see." She moved behind him and herself knelt down too, one knee touching the floor. She reached under him and took hold of the two ends of rope. Her fingers and hands passing between his legs and touching his anus and the base of the tightly-tied testicle-bag gave him further twinges of sheer delight. He avoided looking at the whip whose lash dangled over the edge of the table. Whipping or not, this was much better than the coal-bag shop. But he still wondered a little fearfully what she was going to do with that rope.

In the next second, he understood. He felt her pull on it to bring it taut. Next he felt her wind the ends around his ankles and tie them fast. He was more hepless than he had ever thought it possible to be. The slightest movement of his body, either upwards, forwards or backwards, or sideways, would be made at the risk of castrating himself. He made a very slight tentative movement with his feet. At once his testicle-bag was pulled. Had his movement been greater or more abrupt he would undoubtedly hurt his testicles severely.

He sighed. The position she had put him in was clever, diabolically clever. He supposed she would just stand there and flog him with that whip and he would have to sit still, literally still, and take it. Ordinarily, he imagined, a victim undergoing a whipping would have at least the faint advantage of writhing or squirming. In this position, he would not be able to do either.

She stood up, with a rustle of her robe, and reached for her whip. She ran its lash through her fingers and gazed down at him. There was a wild yet very beautiful light in her eyes. "We're ready," she murmured. "Or at least, I am. Are you?" Her voice was soft, almost caressing.

He looked up and was startled by the expression in her eyes. He had never before seen a woman look like that. It was as though she were in some sort of trance. He shivered slightly, and yet felt a tingle of excitement run through him. "Yes, I'm ready," he said softly. "God help me!"

She moved her position. She drew a very deep breath, slowly, held it in her lungs, and let it out tremulously. She raised her whip. She lashed with a good deal of strength at his shoulder-blades.

He gave a cry, a sharp strangled utterance of astonishment at the agony that ravaged him.

She put her free hand to her breasts beneath her robe. "I love to hear you cry out," she gasped. "Scream! Scream your head off! Nobody will hear you." She struck again... and again... and again...

With his senses in a whirling blaze of pain, he willed himself to sit absolutely still. He knew he would damage himself irreparably under this agony if he once lost control.

He did not cry out again. He gritted his teeth and made no sound other than a deep grunt each time the whip cut into his back.

After she had delivered ten lashes she staggered to the table and leant against it, panting as though she had run up ten flights of stairs. Her hand continued to caress her breasts. Inside them there was a sensation of a thousand tiny needles, each giving repeated pricks of pure ecstasy.

Between her legs, her vulva, wet as though she had stepped from a bath, was pulsating as though it had a life of its own. She moved her hand down and lightly stroked it. The sensation of the thousand tiny needles was at once transferred to her loins.

She stayed where she was waiting to catch her breath, and looking hungrily at the naked, kneeling, hepless body of her victim, his back now a flaming mass of bloody criss-crossed weals.

He knelt in very great pain, still as death, wondering whether she had finished. He realised that he did not very much mind if she had not. The first five lashes had been successively more agonising. But then, it seemed, the zenith of pain must have been reached: the last five lashes had only continued the agony; they had not in any way increased it.

He turned his head and looked at her. He caught his breath as he saw and understood the hunger in her eyes. His heart gave a great leap, despite his pain. She was worth, he decided, any amount of whipping—if he could only have her afterwards. And it seemed that there was a good chance that he was going to. The look in her eyes quite clearly showed that she wanted an orgasm at once.

He was right, but not in the way he expected.

She moved in front of him, her whip still in her hand. She pulled aside the front of her robe, revealing her own nakedness from her neck to her ankles. She took hold roughly of a handful of his hair and thrust his face into her groin. "Send me," she commanded. "Send me with your tongue and lips." She raised her whip and closed her eyes. As she felt his tongue nosing its way towards her vulva, she gave a great shuderring moan of rapture and lashed downwards.

His body flinched mightily as the lashes struck him now from a different angle and regenerated the pain. But, to his dulled surprise, he found that it was becoming less excruciating, more bearable.

He heard her say something.

"What was that?" he asked, lifting his mouth away from her genitals.

She lashed harder. "Don't take your mouth away! I said that when this is over and when I've had a bit of a rest you can do what you want with me." She lashed again. "You'll have earned it."

The orgasm leapt to life at the base of her loins as he put his lips and tongue back to her vulva and vagina. He gently bit her lips—and was rewarded with two savage lashes aimed deliberately down at the crack between his buttocks. This gave him a shaft of a different type of pain and, involuntarily, he jerked himself upwards, forgetting the danger to his testicles. The sensation which he received from them was sufficiently dramatic to prevent his repeating his forgetfulness. He did not repeat his biting of her lips, either. It might cause her to aim again at his crack.

He thrust his tongue as far as he could inside her passage, withdrew it, and thrust again. It came to him that he could put his manacled hands to some use. He removed his face again for a quick moment, thrust his hands up above his head, and put his face back to her genitals through his arms. With his fingers he felt for her breasts. It was not a very comfortable position, after all. He did not dare, however, to move his arms back to where they had been because that would mean he would have to remove his face once more... and this he was loath to do. Two more lashes had been aimed at the crack between his buttocks a moment ago, doubtless for removing his tongue in order to get his hands above his head. So, uncomfortable though the position was, he held it. He caressed first one nipple with all the fingers of both his hands, and then moved to the other nipple.

This had an almost electrical effect on her—and on her approaching orgasm. She was already receiving a tremendous thrill from his lips and tongue; she was also receiving ecstatic pleasure from her simultaneous flagellating his back and bottom at the very time that his tongue and lips were doing their exciting work; and she was having great difficulty in holding the orgasm at bay. She wanted to let it come gradually, slowly—to last a long time. This third excitement of his hands and fingers playing lightly with her nipples utterly destroyed her possibility of delaying the mounting culmination.

She felt it give a great leap. It took command of her. She put the knuckles of her free hand against her teeth and bit them hard. The orgasm increased its force and its fury. She began to moan softly and then, as it seized her and conquered her, she uttered sharp cries of abandoned rapture. She continued to flog with all her strength as long as the culmination pulsed through her, but as the pulses slowly lessened in intensity, so her lashes slowed down and lessened in ferocity. She delivered five or six more even after the pulses had completely stopped—almost as though she were not able to halt the flogging motion of her right arm. Then she dropped the whip to the floor.

She turned to the door. Panting hard, quivering, moaning with exhausted pleasure, she walked unsteadily out of the kitchen.

He listened dejectedly to the bang of the door. He shook his head ruefully. It seemed he would have to stay in this position for a little longer. But she had promised that he could have her—after she had rested—and for some reason that he did not try to analyse he felt certain that she would keep her word.

She returned to the kitchen about half an hour later. She had had a refreshing nap on her bed, and was now completely restored in strength. She was randily ready for the next stage in the day's proceedings. But she was not quite sure what the next stage should be. She would have liked to do a bit more flogging—with one of her other whips, perhaps—but the sight of his lacerated, bleeding back and buttocks made her pause. Perhaps he had had enough... for that day, at any rate. It was, after all, his first full-scale whipping from her.

Later, after she had trained him, he would be able to stand a good deal more.

He was sitting, of course, in the same position—on his ankles. He was sitting quite motionlessly. She felt a twinge of pity for him. She was very well aware of how necessary it is for a man to sit with no movement at all when his testicle-bag has been tied to his ankles.

He said quietly: "Would you please untie me?"

"Untie you? Why?" She thought it would be amusing to tease him for a moment or two. "How do you know I'm not going to give you another whipping?"

"Because I'm in great pain."

She chuckled. "Of course you are! What else is a whipping for?"

"No," he said, shaking his head carefully. "It's not *that* pain. That has almost gone, in fact——" As he said the words he knew he had been unwise.

"Oh, indeed, has it?" she interrupted, moving forward with a rustling swoosh of her robe and picking up the whip from where she had dropped it. "Then it's time for me to give you some more, I think." She stopped and frowned as she saw his face. It was twisted in obvious pain. "But go on. What's the matter?"

"My ankles," he said, between clenched teeth. "I'm sure that the Japanese can sit on their ankles all day—and think nothing of it. But I can't. It's killing me. Please untie me. If only for a little while. You can always tie me up again later if you want to."

Full of contrition, she stooped and untied the knots. "I'm so sorry," she said sincerely. "I didn't think of it." She did not realise the paradox of this feeling of genuine contrition. Like most women who flagellate for the thrill that comes with sexual sadism, she was a warm-hearted creature in everything that was unconnected with sex. She was interested in giving pain only when the pain was in one way or another a part of a sexual act. Since she had already decided not to whip him any more that day, she felt it was most unfair that he should have had to sit for half an hour in an agonisingly uncomfortable position. "I'm so sorry," she repeated. "Do forgive me."

Stiffly, he stood up. He himself appreciated the amusing paradox of her apology. He smiled wryly but said nothing. He stretched his limbs and legs and ankles. The burning pain in his back and buttocks hardly bothered him at all. "Thank you." He grinned at her. "I'll tell you something. Although it was murder, sitting there like that—it was better than being in that rotten coal-bag sewing-shop."

She was opening a packet of cigarettes. She gave him one and lit it. "And the whipping? How was that? Better than the coal-bag shop?"

He hesitated before replying, his eyes on the whip that was once again in her hand. "I didn't think so at first. I thought I'd go off my head with the pain. But later it became more bearable. I suppose I became numb or something." He looked up squarely into her eyes. "So—yes. Yes, it was better than the coal-bags. But are you going to do it again?"

"Am I going to whip you again? Good heavens, yes! Every day."

He shook his head. "I mean now."

She smiled, deciding it was time to stop teasing him. "No, no more today."

He looked at her again. "Do you remember what you said?"

She nodded. "I do."

"Did you mean it?" He began to loosen the knot of the loop round his testicle-bag.

"I did."

He breathed deeply with relief. "I knew I could trust you."

She turned towards the door. "But first you'd better have another bath, and wash that blood off. Put some disinfectant in the water, too. You'll find a bottle of it in the medicine cabinet over the bath."

"Where shall I find you?" The knot came loose. His bag stopped looking like an inflated balloon.

She raised her eyebrows. "In my bedroom, of course. Do you think you're going to make love to me on the kitchen floor?"

He did not hurry over his bath. The hot water was like a soothing balm to his lacerated skin, although it did cause some of the weals to start bleeding again momentarily.

She was lying on her back on her bed, her black silk robe belted around her waist but open all the way down its front. She regarded him with a quiet smile as he climbed on the bed beside her. She reached for his penis. She opened her legs. She pulled him over her. "Don't waste time on any preliminaries," she said. "Take me. I'm randy. I want to have you."

He felt his penis slide deliciously inside her. After all the long months of enforced abstinence he almost swooned with the sweet sensation. He gave a gentle thrust. He experienced another upsurge of sheer delight.

She put her hands to his nipples. She squeezed them. "But make it good," she warned. "Or I'll make you sorry." She stretched herself luxuriously under him. "If you don't make it good, I'll make today's whipping seem like a small child's spanking."

IV

IT'S TIME FOR YOUR MORNING CANING

Two women sat at the large kitchen table, shelling peas.

The table was large because the kitchen was large. It was the kitchen of a manor, in which, in days gone by, a half-dozen servants had been thought to be the minimum required. Today, in the year of grace 1963, the owners of the manor thought themselves extremely lucky to have these two.

One was the cook, a woman of great professional skill but of mean character. The other was the maid, a very pretty girl of about twenty years of age.

The cook glanced up at the clock on the wall. "You'd better go and wake 'em, Gladys. It's almost eight."

Gladys finished shelling the pods that were in her hand. She stood up. "All right," she said. She took off the rubber apron she was wearing and put on, in its place, her crisp white uniform-apron of the mornings.

"And don't take 'alf an hour," said the cook. "You've got a lot to do this morning. You go and wake 'em and get back 'ere quickly. Don't dawdle so."

"What do you mean?" said the other.

"You know what I mean. Takin' 'alf an hour to wake two people."

"Half an hour! What are you talking about? I don't take half an hour."

"Yes you do. These last three or four mornings you've been takin' 'alf an hour. Can't unnerstand it. It's since Mr. and Mrs. Mainwaring went away."

"I just don't know what you're talking about."

The cook leaned forward and glared at the maid. "You do know what I'm takin' about. The last three or four mornings you've been takin' an 'ell of a long time. And with only Miss Margaret and Master Peter to wake up, you oughtn't to take more'n five minutes."

Gladys pouted at her. "What do you want me to do, Cookie? Miss Margaret is very talkative these mornings. She talks her head off. Do you want me to tell her to shut up?"

"Just you get back 'ere quickly," said the cook, frowning darkly.

Gladys leaned herself on the table and glared back at the other. "What *do* you want me to do?" she repeated. "Shall I tell Miss Margaret that Cook doesn't leave me to be more'n five minutes outside the kitchen? Shall I tell her that Cook says she's to shut up so's I can run back to shelling these peas? Is that what you want me to do?"

The cook frowned darkly. "Don't you be cheeky. Just you run along and wake up Miss Margaret and Master Peter, and come on back 'ere directly and get on with your work."

Glads grinned. "All right, then. I'm off—but if Miss Margaret is in the mood to talk her head off again this morning, don't blame *me*. I'll see you when she's finished. Maybe five minutes, maybe half an hour." She looked at the cook and raised her eyebrows. "It could even be an hour, couldn't it?" She chuckled wickedly. "And what would you do about it?" She walked out of the kitchen, leaving the other woman swearing beneath her breath.

Margaret Mainwaring was already awake when she heard the tap on her door. "Good morning, Gladys," she said, hutching herself upon her pillows.

"Good morning, Miss Margaret," said Gladys, as she went to the windows and drew back the curtains. Sunlight flooded the room.

"How's the day?" said Margaret, her eyes still half-closed.

"A lovely day, Miss Margaret."

Margaret Mainwaring stretched her arms high above her pillows. "I'm so glad," she said. She stretched her legs, forcing them to their fullest extremity towards the foot of the bed. "Will you please draw——" She saw that Gladys had gone to the door of the bedroom. "Why are you always in such a hurry these days? It's almost as if you had a train to catch."

With her hand on the handle of the door, Gladys said: "It's Cook, Miss Margaret. If I don't get straight back to the kitchen, I get into hot water."

Margaret Mainwaring nodded her head. She could understand the cook's point of view. A house of this size needed more than a cook and a maid to look after it. "All right, Gladys. I'm sure you have a lot to do in the kitchen. I was going to ask you to draw my bath, but I'll do it myself. You go on back to Cook." She stretched again luxuriously. "Have you woken my brother yet?"

"Not yet, Miss Margaret."

"Off you go then. Go and wake him up."

Gadys left the room and walked along a number of passages towards the room of Peter Mainwaring. He slept in a wing on the opposite side of the house. She walked quickly. Knowing what she was going to do, she felt very excited. Her nerves were tingling.

She tapped lightly on his door and went in, without waiting for him to answer. She locked the door behind her. Then she leant back against it and gazed at him.

He looked very handsome as he lay flat on his back, one arm outstretched over the side of the bed. His pyjama jacket was open. His muscular chest, with a small cluster of blond hairs between his nipples, looked enticing to her. His eyes were closed. He was either still asleep or pretending to be.

She put a hand to her own chest and pressed first her left breast and then her right. She dropped her hand over her groin, and pressed there too. She began to breathe heavily. She was extremely randy.

She moved away from the door. She opened a drawer in a large chest. She took out a long, slender, yellow cane. It had a handle shaped like a U. She ran its length through the fingers of her other hand. She moistened her lips.

"Come on," she said. "You're not asleep." Her voice was a caress.

He opened one eye, and looked quizzically at her with it. "How do you know I'm not?"

"Come on," she repeated. "It's time for your morning caning."

He looked at the cane in her hands. "Why are you such a little beast?"

She raised her eyebrows. "Oh, I'm a little beast, am I? There'll be an extra ten this morning. Twenty in all." She smiled sweetly at him. "That's if you want to have me, of course. If you don't want to have me, or if you're a coward, I'll put this back in the drawer and go back to the kitchen and get on with my work. Cook'll be pleased to see me back quicker than usual."

He threw the bedclothes aside. "Of course I want to have you," he said grumpily. "But it seems to be getting more and more expensive. Twenty, for God's sake!"

"You shouldn't call me a little beast."

He lay still for a moment and then kicked all the bedclothes to the floor. He put his hands to his pyjama trousers, opened the slit and brought out his penis. It was mightily erected. He massaged it gently, his eyes on hers.

"Pee-pride!" she said. "Go and get rid of it. Let's have a normal stiffness."

"It's not pee-pride," he answered, continuing to massage the stiffness. "I peed about a quarter of an hour ago. This is very normal."

She moved to the bed, sat down, and took the penis in her free hand. "Then it's very nice." She lowered her head and put her lips to its tip. His body went taut with longing. She looked up at him momentarily. "Yes, you want to have me, I can see! You want me very much."

"Yes," he said, with a sharp intake of breath. "Very much indeed. Why don't you forget the beastly caning and let me have you now." He reached upwards to seize her.

She eluded him quickly and stood up. She laughed gaily. "Forget the beastly caning! What *do* you say?" She ran the length of the cane through her fingers again. "Beastly caning, indeed! It's wonderful thing, a caning. A wonderful, marvellous, thrilling, exciting thing." She laughed again. "To *give* a caning, anyway. I don't know whether it's so wonderful, marvellous and thrilling to receive one."

"It is not," he said emphatically. "It's bloody murder."

She reached forward and took hold of his penis again. "But you want me so much that you'd accept any amount of murder, wouldn't you? Not simply twenty. A silly, cissy little twenty. You'd accept a hundred, wouldn't you?"

He looked up at her with alarm in his eyes. "Of course not. You're crazy!"

She studied him, wondering whether to tell him that

he must now accept a full hundred or not have her. Then she remembered the cook. She simply wouldn't have the time. "No," she said. "Don't be afraid. Only twenty today. But one of these days, when I have more time, it's going to be a hundred." She glanced at the watch on his wrist. "Time's getting on, too. I'll get it in the neck from Cook." She looked at him mischievously. "Do you know where she thinks I am?"

"No. Where?"

"With your sister. I tell her that Miss Margaret is very talkative these mornings, and I have to stay and chat with her."

He laughed. "That's as good an excuse as any."

She tapped his penis lightly with the cane. "Come on. Take your trousers off."

He sighed elaborately, but obeyed her without argument. He untied the cord of his pyjamas and slipped the trousers over his ankles. He kicked them to the floor.

"All right," she said. "Turn over. Show me what your poor bottom looks like."

With another sigh, he turned over onto his stomach.

She breathed in deeply, with great satisfaction, as she saw the condition of his buttocks. She had caned him soundly the last four mornings, giving him ten of the hardest strokes of her quite strong right arm. She had each time made his buttocks bleed profusely. And now the sight of the damage done by the thrashings of four mornings made her feel more than ever randy, and more than ever sadistic. She wanted to lash so hard with her cane that he would be unable to sit down for a month. She wanted to make the blood run fast.

She raised her cane. It flashed down across the lacerated flesh. Blood spurted at once. He gave a strangled cry and bit deeply into his pillow.

"No," she said. "This won't do. Your bed will look as though a murder has been done on it. Get up." She looked around the bedroom. She pointed with the cane, already shining with the blood of her first lash, at the chair standing before his desk. "Go and bend over that."

"Hold on a mo'," he protested. "That's not in our agreement."

She looked surprised. "What's not?"

"Bending over a chair."

She looked more than ever surprised. "Why? What's so bad about bending over a chair?"

"It hurts more," he said, frowning self-consciously. "We said that I'd only have to lie here and be caned—if I want to have you. We didn't say anything about bending over a chair."

She nodded her head reflectively. It was quite true. They had not said anything about bending over a chair...

That first morning, four days ago now, she had tapped on the door of his bedroom as usual, had waited until she heard his muffled "Come in," and had entered the room to complete the formality of waking him. It was not necessary to draw his curtains, for he liked to sleep with both curtains and windows open. All she usually did was to say, "Good morning, Master Peter. It's eight o'clock." And then she would leave the room, giving a deep sigh of inhibited longing, as she closed the door again, at his twenty-year-old masculine attraction. And she would go back to the kitchen in a condition of quivering randiness, wishing that she could do something about the wretched situation. She despaired, however, of fulfilling her wish because her randiness was not for copulation: it was for flagellation. Gladys was a born sadist. She knew, therefore, that the situation was not very promising for her... How could she ever hope to flagellate Master Peter!

That morning, however, four days ago, had been unexpectedly propitious. As she entered the room to say the usual "Good morning, Master Peter," his bed-clothes had been flung aside because the room was warm. His penis, mightily erected, had been thrusting itself through the slit of his pyjama-trousers. His left hand lay across his groin, its fingers playing idly up and down the centre nerve of the penis. His eyes were closed. Although he had called "Come in," he was still half-asleep. She came into the room so softly that he did not hear her.

He opened his eyes as he heard her catch her breath. He quickly pulled away his hand. He blinked twice, and then felt completely awake. He blushed. Then he pretended to cough, turning himself away from her. He grunted something unintelligible.

Some intuition told her that an opportunity was being offered to her. She hesitated for only a moment. Then she moved to his bedside and sat down. She reached her hand over and took hold of his penis.

His body gave a mighty tremor but he said nothing.

Her fingers ran up and down the hard erection. "Is that nice?" she said, softly.

He did not answer.

"Is it nice?" she repeated.

He made a great effort to overcome his embarrassment. He turned and lay on his back again, but he avoided her eyes. "Yes, but it will be nicer if I go and pee."

She said, in great surprise. "If you *pee!* What has that got to do with what I'm doing to you?"

"This is pee-pride." It was as though he wanted to excuse his erection.

"What's pee-pride? I don't understand you." She took her hand away from his penis, but remained sitting where she was. "What are you talking about?"

"This stiff that you've just touched."

She looked at him and said patiently. "Master Peter, I don't understand what you're talking about."

He grinned suddenly at her, a very attractive grin that made her heart jump up and then turn over.

"Little Gladys," he said. "You're very sweet—and very innocent. Are you a virgin?"

She hesitated, and then said bluntly: "No, I'm not."

"Good," he said. "That makes things a good deal easier." He lay back against the pillows and regarded her appreciatively.

She knew very well what he meant, but she said, "I don't know what you're talking about. Let's get things straight, one by one. What does pee-pride mean?"

He laughed. He was rapidly losing the last of his embarrassment. "You don't know? Well, it's like this. Men often wake up with a stiff like this, but it doesn't mean anything at all except that they want to pee."

She frowned. "First time I've heard that. Why does wanting to pee make 'em stiff?"

He shook his head. "I don't know."

"You mean if you go and pee, the stiff'll go away?"

"Yes, it always does. As soon as I pee."

She thought about this for a moment or two, and suddenly felt angry. She stood up. "In that case," she said icily, "I'll get back to my work."

He caught her hand. "What's the matter?"

"Nothing's the matter." She tried to disengage her hand from his.

"Yes, there is. What is it?" He knew what it was, but he was too young to see that he was being foolish with his persistent questioning.

"I thought——" She stopped in mid-sentence. "Let me go. I must go."

He swung his legs to the floor and stood up beside her. "Please don't go. Please sit down for a moment. You're angry about something." A flash of wisdom came to his mind. "I know perfectly well what it is. You just sit there for a moment, and I'll show you something—and everything'll be all right." He pushed her down on to the side of the bed. "You'll stay there?"

She was still very angry, but she nodded.

"Good. I'm now going to pee this pee-pride away." He walked quickly to his bathroom, took his penis in his hands and urinated luxuriously. The stiffness disappeared. The penis resumed its normal flaccid condition. It stayed like that for a moment, and then, as he thought of the girl sitting on his bed, it began to rise once more. He waited until it was fully erected. He went back into the bedroom with it swinging from side to side as he walked. He went up close to her. He reached for her hands and guided them to the stiff flesh and muscle. "I didn't explain it at all well," he said quietly. "I peed. The false stiff went away. Now I have this. And this isn't at all false."

"Why should I care?" she said huffily. She felt that she had been insulted in some way. She could not understand how, but she was sure there had been some affront to her as a girl, and all the prickly withers of her class were standing upright. She pulled her hands away as he tried to guide them to his penis.

He sighed. He sat down beside her. "Let's start again," he said patiently. "Something I said made you angry. I don't know what it was, but I'm sorry."

She tossed her head. "Why should I be angry? If you want to play with yourself in your sleep, it's nothing to do with me." But she did not attempt to stand up, despite the umbrage in her voice. An instinct was beginning to tell her that she was going too far. Perhaps she had indeed been affronted in some peculiar way, but she ought to ignore it—if she wanted to seize on the opportunity that she sensed was in her hands. So she sighed, too, with a lift and fall of her shoulders, and turned and smiled at him. "All right, Master Peter," she said, in a cool but more friendly tone of voice, "I don't myself know what it was, but let's forget it, shall we? It's silly to quarrel." She moved one of her hands and took hold of his penis lightly. "And you say that *this* isn't pee-pride."

He felt a sensation of great relief. "No, it's certainly not pee-pride."

She regarded the stiff flesh and muscle curiously. "How do I know? It looks to me the same as it was before you went to pee."

"Squeeze it. Squeeze it hard."

She glanced at him and nodded. This was the sort of thing she liked doing. It was a sort of violence. And violence in any shape or form was her god. "All right," she said, beginning to apply pressure with her fingers. "I'd love to squeeze it. But tell me why. What will it prove?"

A sweet sensation began to go through him as he felt the beginning pressure of her fingers. "You can't squeeze a pee-pride."

She increased the pressure. "You *can't?* Why can't you?"

He caught his breath. She was beginning to hurt him. "I don't know. You just can't."

"But you can squeeze a normal stiff?" She was beginning to enjoy herself. She shifted her fingers quickly so that her fingernails should sink into the erected penis. She squeezed harder. "Like that?"

"Yes!" he gasped, beginning to squirm under the pain of her fingernails, now biting deeply into his flesh. "You—couldn't—squeeze like that—if this—were—just —pee-pride." He wished she would stop, but his sense of manliness prevented him from crying out. "It would—just—break off!"

She called upon all the strength of her hand. "But now it's not pee-pride, and it won't break off, eh?" Her wrist was beginning to ache with the strain that she was putting on her muscles.

He sat with his head thrown back, his mouth wide open. He would have to scream, any second now, for her to stop. The pain was excruciating. But at the same time, there was—unaccountably, mysteriously—a sort of pleasure at the base of the anguish. He pushed his knuckles against his teeth and bit them. If she didn't stop she would injure him for ever...

At the moment he was ready to scream, she stopped. She drew a deep, quivering breath. She took her hand away. Her finger-nails had made deep, angry marks in the flesh. "Ooooh!" she murmured.

"That was a bit rough," he said shakily.

"You told me to squeeze you, didn't you?"

"I didn't think you'd have so much strength."

She laughed. "You didn't, eh?" She looked at her hand. "It comes from wringing the washing." She looked up into his eyes. "But that was with my left hand. Shall I do it again with my right? It might be better."

He stood up abruptly. "No, for God's sake, no! That was quite enough to show anyone that this isn't pee-pride."

"Oh yes," she said. She had begun to forget that the squeezing had primarily been intended to prove that the erection was a normal one. "Of course." She took a deep breath. The moment had come for the next step. "You want to have me, Master Peter, I suppose?"

He was a little taken aback by the directness of her question. He did not know that she was in a hurry, afraid of what the cook would say about her having been so long away from the kitchen. "Yes," he said. "I want you very much. I've wanted you ever since you came into the house. When was that? Six months ago?"

"Seven."

"We've wasted a lot of time." He was very surprised that she was offering herself, as it were, on a plate. He had long wanted to do something about her, particularly each morning when she wakened him, but he had not had the requisite courage. And he had heard of the terrible trouble that had come to a fellow-undergraduate who had copulated with a maid in his household... But he did not think now of the possibility of terrible trouble for himself. Here was this ravishingly attractive maid offering herself to him on a plate. He did not even consider the possibility of refusing her. He simply wondered what the next step should be. Should he push her down on her back? Or should he lie down himself?

She answered the question for him. She took hold of the cord of his pyjama-trousers and pulled it. The trousers fell around his ankles. "There!" she said. "Isn't that better?"

He thought that he should do the same to her. He took her hand and pulled her to her feet. He lifted the hem of her skirt.

She moved away from him. "Not so fast, Master Peter."

He blinked at her. "What do you mean?"

She regarded him seriously. "You want to have me, don't you?"

"Yes." He thought it was a silly waste of time to go through this again. "Yes, of course I do. You know it."

"And it's quite a good time, really—with your father and mother away as they are."

"What have they got to do with it?" he asked, frowning slightly with puzzlement. "Why should it be quite a good time—just because they're away? Their room is miles away, in any case."

She nodded slowly and mysteriously. "You'll see why, in a minute." She took hold of his penis again. "You say you want me. Okay, you can have me. But on one condition."

He squirmed with the pleasure of her fingers. "What condition?"

"You'll be very surprised."

"I'll risk it."

She ran her middle finger lightly up and down the central nerve of the penis. "And I doubt whether you'll accept it." And she thought to herself: Oh God, *make* him accept it! Make me so desirable to him that he'll accept it.

He said, with the beginning of impatience in his voice: "Do stop being mysterious, Gladys. What is this condition of yours? Tell me."

She gave his penis the most exciting sort of caress that she could. She forced herself to be calm. The great moment had arrived. She would tell him her condition. "If you want to have me," she said deliberately and very clearly, "you must take a thrashing from me first."

"A *what?*"

"You heard correctly, Master Peter."

"A thrashing?"

"Yes, a thrashing. Ten of the best—with the cane that is in your mother's room. She has it to beat her furs with. But I'll use it to beat your bottom with—if you want me badly enough." She stole a look at his face. "That's why I said it's a good time," she added parenthetically. "Since your mother's away, I can go and borrow her cane. If she weren't away, I couldn't borrow it."

He had been listening to her without believing his ears. "But why? *Why?* Why should you want to beat my bottom? What have I done wrong to you?" He remembered her anger during the misunderstanding about his pee-pride, but he rejected the thought. This was not at all connected with that misunderstanding. "I don't get it. Tell me why you want to beat my bottom."

"I like thrashing men," she said simply. And then, with a quick intake of breath, she went on: "I like to make 'em lie flat on their faces and take my thrashing. And I like to use a nice swishy cane on their bottoms—the sort of cane your mother has in her room for her furs." She gave an aggressive sigh. "That's what I like. Are you going to take it, and have me after? Or do I just go straight back to the kitchen?" And she prayed: Dear God, *make* him take it!

He ran his fingers over his naked buttocks. "Ten you say?"

"Yes, ten. But ten of the best." Her heart began to thump. It seemed as though he was going to accept it. She wondered whether she ought to have added that "of the best." But she at once retrospectively approved of having added it. Let him agree—but let him know the full extent of what he was agreeing to. If he didn't, he would start making a fuss in the middle of her enjoyment.

He stood silently, considering the matter. Ten strokes of a cane did not seem too high a price to pay for having such a girl as this. In the not-so-distant past, at his public school, he had often received ten strokes of a cane. No, that was not true. They had usually been six. Practically never ten. But the six had been given by a master, a man, with a man's muscles. These ten would be given by a girl, with a girl's muscles... He suddenly remembered the tremendous strength that she had shown when squeezing his penis, and he shivered inwardly. But he would be lying down on the bed. She had said: "I like to make 'em lie flat on their faces." That was a great advantage for him. He would not be bending over a chair, or a table, or anything like that. He would be lying with his buttocks relaxed, and that would be a great deal less painful, he remembered, than bending over. Just so long as he could lie on his tummy for her thrashing, he could take it and sing a song.

He grinned at her. "Okay, you—you—what's the word they call people like you?"

She smiled back at him. "Sadist?"

"Yes, that's the word."

"So you do know something about it."

He shrugged his shoulders. "Not really. I've read things here and there. But I've never taken it seriously."

She chuckled. "You're going to take it very seriously now." She went to the door. "I'll go and get that delicious cane of your mother's. And I'll come back and give you ten of the best. And then you can do whatever you want to me, and I'll love it."

All that had been four days ago. Now she stared at him as he repeated his protest. "We didn't say anything about bending over chairs. In fact, I very clearly remember you saying that you like to make people lie flat on their faces."

"Yes," she said. "But I don't want your sheets to look as though someone has bled to death on 'em."

"Don't hit me so hard, then."

She said crisply: "I should have thought these last mornings would have taught you something about a sadist, Master Peter. It's a very silly thing, what you've just said. I just can't hit you less hard. I have to hit you with all my force or I don't get any pleasure."

He wondered what to say. He could, of course, tell her to go and take the next bus to hell. But if he did that he would lose these wonderful morning copulations. *Wonderful* copulations? *Were* they so wonderful, since he had to pay so dearly in blood and pain for them? He considered the matter seriously and then had to admit that they were not only wonderful but fully worth the blood and pain. He would go on taking whatever she wanted to give him.

He climbed off the bed. "All right. Have it your own way. But"—he glanced sharply at her—"you might forget that other ten, mightn't you? It's going to be blue bloody murder—bending over that chair."

"No, it's not," she said sweetly. "It's going to be

red bloody murder. Very red, and very, very bloody." She looked down at the carpet. "It's a good thing this is the colour it is. It won't show your blood." She swished the cane ominously through the air. "Come on. Bend over that chair. We haven't got all day."

He bent his body over the back of the chair. "Lower," she said. "Put your hands on the seat. Go on, lower. Put your palms flat on the seat." He ran her hand over his buttocks again. She agitated her finger-tips into the blood she had brought. She lifted these fingers to her lips and licked the blood away with the tip of her tongue. She began to feel faint with excitement. "Twenty of the best," she murmured. "Here we go." She raised her cane high.

He exclaimed. "What do you mean, twenty? It should be only nineteen. You gave me one on the—" The word bed was convulsively swallowed as the cane slashed across his tightened backside. He gave a howl of pain.

"Sssshhh," she said sternly. "If you make that sort of noise we'll be found out and then you won't get what you're paying for." She lashed again with all her force. The cane struck into exactly the same weal as it had made the previous stroke. Globules of blood rose into the air and fell in a shower on to the maroon-coloured carpet. She let out her breath tremulously. She re-arranged her stance and began to count as she lashed. "Three—four—five—six—seven—eight—nine—ten!" She put a hand to her head. Her brain was reeling. She felt that she would drop to the carpet in a dead faint. Into her swimming senses came the exciting thought that, if she did fall to the carpet, she would fall on to a dampness of blood that she had put there.

In a blaze of agony, he stood erect. He looked at her through something like a mist. He seized the cane from her hand and threw it across the room.

He reached out with his other hand and took hold of her hair. He pulled her abruptly to him.

"Oh yes," she breathed, in a long, shuddering sigh. "Take me now, Peter. Never mind the other ten. I'll give you them tomorrow morning." She grabbed his penis and squeezed with all her might.

He swung her off her feet and began to carry her towards the bed.

"No!" she said urgently. "You're covered with blood. Not the bed. The floor, for God's sake!"

He paused for a second and then placed her, on her back, upon the blood-damp carpet. He lifted her skirt and felt for her knickers. He gave an impatient pull. The material tore.

She said, in a tone of great satisfaction. "That'll be *another* ten tomorrow morning, my Peter." As had happened on the previous four mornings, her use of the word Master in front of his name disappeared after her cane had cut into his buttocks. She felt his weight coming down on her. "So that'll be thirty lovely strokes I'll give you tomorrow. OoooHhh!" His penis, having nosed briefly against her sex-drenched vulva-lips, thrust itself hard into her wet vagina-passage. "OOOHHH!" she cried, in ecstatic abandon. "Oh God, where's my cane? Oh God, oh God! I want to thrash you now, as you're going in me..." She continued to moan hysterically and rapturously.

But when her orgasm approached, and came up to her, and finally took her in its honeyed grasp to shake her into a quivering surrender, she had no thoughts of sadism, of canes and blood and pain. She felt her very self merge and flow into him, and become one with him.

And she was fulfilled, translated, and thoroughly satisfied.

V

GUILTY OF OBJECTIONABLE BEHAVIOUR

Saunders, second mate of the tanker "Santa Maria", lay flat on his back on a camp-bed on the deck just below the bridge. He had a canvas awning rigged above him against the heat and the rays of the scorching Arabian sun. He had tried to take his siesta in his cabin, but the temperature there—over one hundred and thirty degrees Fahrenheit—had driven him up on to the deck. Here the temperature was one hundred and twenty degrees.

He was wearing only his pants. He lay, sweating and gasping with the intolerable heat, and stretched his long legs as though, by stretching them, he might in some way alleviate his discomfort. The action had a contrary effect. A new rush of sweat drenched his whole body. The sun struck down through the canvas awning like a welder's flame through a piece of tissue-paper. Its glare burned through his closed eyelids, giving him the impression that he was looking up at a million brightly burning stars. He groaned, and turned over on his side. The movement brought a fresh rush of sweat over his legs and arms and chest and back. It ran down the side of his head and filled his ears and his eyes. He groaned again.

"You find it hot?" said a voice beside him, with light irony.

Saunders opened his eyes and saw that his Captain was standing beside his camp-bed. "Don't you?" he said sourly.

"I used to," said the Captain reflectively. "But I've got myself accustomed to it."

"Shall we be able to get away tomorrow?"

"I hope so. We'll finish the bow and the middle tanks by ten o'clock tonight. And we'll have the stern tanks full before dawn. Yes, we should be away before breakfast."

"Christ, I hope so."

The Captain regarded the younger man. "It'll be better in a few hours. It gets a lot cooler after the sun goes down."

"That's good news," said Saunders. "I'll be able to go ashore a bit."

The Captain frowned. "Do so, if you want to. But be careful how you behave. This country is very mediaeval in its laws. Don't go and do anything wrong."

Saunders grinned. "I need a woman. Is there anything wrong in that?"

The Captain frowned again. "Depends on the woman. If she's a whore, it's all right. If she's not, you may find yourself in trouble."

"Come off it, Skip. A woman's a woman, anywhere in the world. And I don't feel particularly interested in Arab whores." Saunders wiped his hand across his face and flung the sweat to the deck. "We've been at sea too long for a whore to be any good. A whore is just a quick poke. I need a *good* poke."

"You'd better be satisfied with a quick one," said the Captain shortly. "Or I can see that this ship will be sailing without its second mate."

Saunders shook his head. "Don't worry, Skip. I can look after myself."

"I hope so," said the Captain seriously. "Just remember what I told you about this place. It still has mediaeval laws—and very mediaeval ideas about punishment."

The oil-rich Kingdom of Gubadan, in whose capital city the tanker "Santa Maria" was at that moment taking on board her cargo of crude oil, is indeed mediaeval in its laws. It is a country of some two million people, half of whom live in the capital. This is a city of wide boulevards and high concrete buildings. It is a thriving metropolis with virtually no poverty. Oil has given a high standard of living even to those who once were beggars. It is said that every fourth person owns a car, and many of the cars are Cadillacs and Lincolns.

The King is the absolute ruler. There is no parliament, there are no elected representatives of the people. Government affairs are carried on by "ministers" but these are appointed by the King, and they are answerable only to him. He himself holds the portfolios of foreign affairs defence and finance. His son, the Crown Prince, is responsible for roads and transport. Since, however, there are few roads outside the capital, and most of the nation's transport is carried out by camel-caravans, which continue to operate as they have operated for thousands of years, there is little for the prince to do. He spends most of his time abroad.

The Princess Makasile, the King's only daughter, is a more interesting person than the Crown Prince. An incredibly lovely creature of twenty-eight years of age, she has been acting as the Minister of Justice for the past three years. And, as Minister of Justice, she is automatically also the principal judge of the kingdom.

She was educated abroad at a famous school and later at an even more famous finishing school, where she perfected her command of English, French and German. Reluctant to return at once to the restricted life of royalty in her own country, she succeeded in persuading her father to allow her to enter a university for further studies. She chose to read law, not because she was interested in law but because she had to read something. Four years later, as a qualified Barrister-at-Law, she returned to Gubadan. Within six months she persuaded her father that she was better qualified to become his Minister of Justice than anyone else in the land. It was a long battle because the King is conservative in his ideas, and he does not approve of women interfering in men's work. In the face of Makasile's persistent cajolery, however, he gave in at last, and three years ago he appointed her his Minister of Justice and principal judge.

She proceeded at once to abolish slavery and to reform certain parts of an undeniably barbaric penal code. She did not, however, abolish punishment by flogging—and, sometimes, the bastinado.

The Princess Makasile is a firm believer in the corrective benefits of flogging. Or that, at least, is what she says. Some of her detractors have suggested that she has a more personal interest in its effects. There are even whispers that she has her own punishment-room in the palace, in which criminals are sometimes flogged by her own hand. No one is certain of this, of course, because no proof could ever come to light. If it is true, then certainly some of the prison guards and some of the Palace servants must know about it: someone, after all, has to deliver the prisoner to the Princess's private punishment-room. There is no danger, however, of anyone's corroborating it. The informer's head would assuredly fall. In the Kingdom of Gubadan execution remains a common punishment, and not only the Monarch but also the Crown Prince and the Princess Makasile have the power to order it, summarily. The Princess's reforms have not included the abolition of this royal prerogative.

Saunders went ashore that night with the third mate and the second engineer. The dreadful heat of the day had disappeared but it was still too warm for them to wear their uniform jackets. They set off, like ordinary seamen, in shirt sleeves and white duck trousers.

The third mate had been in the capital once before. He led them to a sort of night club which had been built beneath a big block of offices in the centre of the city.

The three of them ordered a bottle of whisky each and a siphon of soda to share among them. Within a minute three quite pretty dancing-girls arrived at the table. Invited to sit, they sat down and proceeded to pay more attention to Saunders, who was thirty years of age and very good looking, than to the other two men, who were older and relatively nondescript to look at.

The second engineer laughed good naturedly. "You've made a big hit," he said to Saunders. "You'd better take your pick. They're offering it to you on a plate."

Saunders grinned. "The dark one is the best. Let's toss for her."

The girl he was referring to, a dark-skinned creature with a trace of the Ethiopian in her features, stood up and came up to him. She sat down on his knees, kissed him lightly on his cheek and put an arm round his neck. "I understand English very well. And nobody's going to toss for me. I give myself to whom I choose."

He put his arm round her waist and hugged her. "Thank you for the compliment. Have some whisky?"

As he filled her glass and his own, he told himself that he ought to be well-enough pleased with the situation. She was a pretty thing, and she obviously liked him. She would make a good poke. Nevertheless she was a professional, and Saunders had an ache to sleep with a woman who was not a whore or a near-whore. He wanted to have a romantic adventure. He was still too inexperienced with the ways of the East to realise that it would be extremely difficult, if not downright dangerous, to find such an adventure. He determined to finish his bottle of whisky with this girl, give her a tip, and leave his shipmates to their own devices. He would go off on his own and try to find what he wanted.

Two hours later he left the night club. His tip to the girl had been more than generous, but it had only slightly soothed her sense of insult. He went in the direction of the Palace Hotel. There he might find a European girl, the daughter, perhaps, of one of the foreign oil executives in the capital. Or, if he were lucky, he might find a Gubadanian girl of the modern emancipated circle, one who would have been educated abroad and would therefore have no nonsense with veils and so forth. An adventure with a Gubadanian girl, he told himself, might be a very nice thing to have.

He entered the bar of the Palace Hotel, a large room with a highly polished parquet floor and glittering chandeliers hanging from the expensively panelled ceiling. Because of the season, with its attendant heat, there were no carpets or rugs on the floor, and the usual heavy silk damask curtains had been removed from the windows. He made his way to an empty table, ordered a double whisky and soda, and surveyed the room.

There were forty or fifty people in the bar. At first it seemed, to his disappointment, that every woman had an escort, but then he saw a beautiful girl sitting alone on a low settee at the other end of the bar.

He waited for his whisky to arrive. He got up, glass in hand, and made his way towards the girl. As he approached her, a silence fell over the bar. People stared at him with surprise on their faces. He had already drunk the better part of a bottle of whisky, and his perceptions were dulled. He did not notice the silence and the stares. Nor did he notice that there were two glasses on the table before the girl. If he had done so, he might have realised that the girl was not alone, that her escort had obviously left her for a moment to go to the lavatory or the telephone.

He made a gallant bow and said: "A beautiful lady like you should not be sitting alone. May I sit down and introduce myself?" Without waiting for an answer, he sat down on the settee beside her.

The girl, an aristocratic looking Gubadanian, looked at him with amusement. She said nothing. The silence in the bar became intense, electric.

A man appeared in the doorway, and stopped in his tracks when he saw Saunders. He frowned angrily. He was a tall, slim man of about forty, in European clothes but quite clearly a Gubadanian. He let his hands fall to his sides, his fists half clenched. He began to walk, with the slow lithe tread of a panther, towards the settee.

The girl glanced towards him. The amusement deepened in her eyes. Saunders followed her look. When he saw the approaching man, his first feeling was one of disappointment. He would have no romantic adventure with this girl, after all. His second feeling was one of anger with himself. He had drunk too much whisky and was making a fool of himself. He sighed and stood up as the man came up to the settee.

"I have made a mistake," he said quietly. "I hope you will accept my apologies."

The man swung his fist back and struck hard. Saunders tried to dodge the blow but his whisky-dulled reactions were too slow. It caught him full on the point of his chin. He went over like a nine-pin.

He lay still for a moment, anger filling his mind. He had apologised, hadn't he? What right had this man to hit him so unexpectedly? He gathered his strength and began to get to his feet. He would take back his apology with his own fists. He did not notice two policemen, summoned by the frightened hotel-manager, running into the bar. He became aware of them as he finally stood erect, and as they grabbed his arms, twisted them behind his back, and hustled him out of the hotel. On the pavement, while one of them blew a whistle, he struggled free. The other drew his truncheon and used it swiftly, accurately, and hard.

Saunders dropped to the pavement like a discarded sack. When the police truck arrived he was still totally unconscious.

The following morning, the Public Prosecutor telephoned the palace and asked to speak to the Princess Makasile. He had had strict orders to report directly to her any charges that were to be made against a foreign national.

After paying the usual courteous respects, he said: "Highness, there is an Englishman for punishment this morning. The second mate of a tanker. He committed a nuisance in the Palace Hotel bar last night."

"What did he do?" asked the Princess.

"He accosted the wife of the Shaikh of Khan."

"Oh dear," said the Princess. "Did he really? That's rather serious."

"Yes, Highness," said the Prosecutor expressionlessly. "It is serious. The Shaikh was very angry." He spoke in an expressionless tone because he was sure what her next remark would be.

There was a slight pause. "I'd better deal with him myself," she said. "We mustn't offend the Shaikh. On the other hand, he's a foreigner and we mustn't go too far. Yes, send him to the private court. I'll consider what is the best thing to do with him."

The Prosecutor smiled. He had been quite right. "Very well, Highness. I will transfer him to your private jurisdiction."

The Princess put down her telephone and wondered what sort of man this Englishman was. To have accosted the wife of the Shaikh of Khan showed, at least, that he had good taste in women. It also showed, however, that he must be a reckless sort of person, with little or no knowledge of the laws of Gubadan. Were he a Gubadanian, the punishment for such an offence would have to be very drastic indeed, if only to placate the Shaikh. He was an Englishman, however, and that meant that the punishment would have to be less drastic. It was always a fuss to have to deal with notes and protests.

She wondered how old he was, and what he looked like. She would have liked to ask the Prosecutor, but that would not have done. She would soon see for herself, though. Her private court was due to sit at eleven o'clock.

Saunders, with handcuffs on his wrists and chains on his feet, was led to the dock in what seemed to him to be an obvious, but very small, court-room. His head was aching both from the whisky he had drunk and from the crack over his skull that he had received from the policeman's truncheon. He looked around the room. The judge's chair was empty. On either side of it sat a black-robed Gubadanian. Below the Bench a clerk was idly reading through a sheaf of papers. There was no one else.

A bell rang. Everybody stood up.

A door opened and a woman in a black silk robe walked quickly to the Judge's chair. She sat down. The others bowed deeply to her and sat down too.

Saunders looked at her in astonishment. She seemed to be about his own age, or perhaps two or three years younger, and was extremely beautiful. Her hair, dark and silky, was dressed in a style which was seemingly casual but which had obviously been set with great care. Her eyes were large and alive as she studied him. Her cheekbones were high, aristocratic—but very feminine. Her mouth and lips had a sensual attraction that took his breath away. He reflected that, though he was obviously in great trouble, it was a trouble that was not without interest. It was even exciting to be at the mercy of a Judge like this.

The clerk stood up again, bowed once more, and read from the sheaf of papers in his hand. Since he spoke in Gubadanian, Saunders understood nothing. He seemed to speak for a very long time. Saunders, remembering the lightning-like speed of the events of the previous night, wondered how it was possible for the charge against him to be so lengthy. At last it came to an end. The clerk bowed again and sat down.

There was a silence.

Saunders gazed at the Judge and, despite his headache, wished that he could take her to bed.

The Princess looked at the prisoner and read the thoughts that were so openly expressed by his eyes. She was neither offended nor annoyed. With satisfaction she saw that he was young and attractive.

"You are in grave trouble," she said in English. "What have you to say for yourself?"

Saunders wondered how to address her. Your Honour, perhaps? Or Your Worship? The clerk settled his doubts for him. "Answer Her Highness," he said in English.

Oh! thought Saunders. Her Highness! This becomes more and more interesting. He bowed his head slightly. "I am extremely sorry, Your Highness," he said, in a quiet tone. "I suppose I was drunk."

"Why didn't you stay in some seaman's bar, then?

Do you think you can behave in that way in a place like the Palace Hotel? And do you think you can insult a noblewoman in such a place?"

"I didn't know she was a noblewoman, Your Highness. And I certainly didn't insult her. If anything, I paid her a compliment."

The Princess repressed a smile. She gazed at him pensively. She began to find him more and more attractive. She forced her voice to be stern. "In a comparable bar in your own country, would you have crossed the room and accosted a woman who was sitting alone?"

He realised that, in honesty, he would have to admit he would not.

"Answer Her Highness," said the clerk peremptorily. He shook his head. "No, I must say I wouldn't."

"Then you admit you are guilty of objectionable behaviour." She said this as a statement, not as a question. Nevertheless, she seemed now to be waiting for him to say something.

"I suppose I am," he said ruefully. Perhaps he would get off more lightly if he admitted it without excuses and arguments. "And I am very sorry. I should like to apologise to the lady in question."

"I doubt if you'll ever have that chance," said the Princess grimly. "Now, what am I to do with you? Her husband is demanding that you be sent to a labour camp."

Saunders felt himself go cold. He had heard something of the labour camps in Gubadan. They might have abolished slavery, but they had not abolished the camps, and the clock there had stood still for over a thousand years.

He heard himself stammering. "But, Your Highness, what is he talking about? All I did was to admire his wife. That is not such a crime, surely?"

"It is, in this country." She regarded him thoughtfully. She was not thinking about how to punish him.

95

She had decided that as soon as she saw him. She was congratulating herself for deciding to have him brought to her private court. It would have been a great pity to miss him. He was obviously very frightened by what she had said about the labour camp. It would be amusing to keep him in suspense for a little while longer. "You seem scared," she said slowly.

He looked into her eyes. "Yes," he said frankly. "If you'll forgive me, I've heard stories about the labour camps in this country."

"Why didn't you think of them last night, before doing what you did?" She realised that she was behaving disgracefully as a Judge, bandying words back and forth with a prisoner, just because he was an attractive man.

"But I told you," he said desperately. "I didn't realised you had such—such strict laws." He was going to say crazy laws, but he stopped himself in time. "And I must ask to be allowed to speak with my Consul."

"That will not do you any good."

"But it is my right. It is international law."

The Princess smiled. She was enjoying herself very much. "So you are a lawyer, too?" She glanced at the clerk below her. He seemed to be carved of stone. She wondered what he was thinking. The two magistrates on either side of her spoke no English, and so they could be ignored. For the sake of her reputation with the clerk, however, she had better bring this to an end. "You shall not be sent to a labour camp. You are a foreigner, and traditionally we are lenient in our treatment of foreigners."

Saunders breathed a sigh of relief.

She saw the sigh and wondered how he was going to react to her next words. "You must, however, have a punishment of some sort. I shall order the most lenient."

He held his breath as she paused.

"You shall be flogged," she said, and felt her heart give an excited little jump at the thought of it. "Now, let me see. Shall it be a major flogging, or an intermediate one, or a minor one?" She looked into his eyes and enjoyed the expression of shocked incredulity that began to appear there. "I think it must be a major flogging." She nodded at the clerk. He wrote something at the foot of her paper. She glanced again at Saunders, rose from her chair, and swept gracefully out of the court.

In the sweltering heat of the afternoon, Saunders lay on the wooden bed in his cell, sweated, and wondered whether his ship had left. It was highly doubtful that the captain would have waited for him. What had been his words? "Or I can see that this ship will be sailing without its second mate." The warning had been clear enough. The ship must by now have sailed.

He sighed. So he was to be flogged. And it was to be what she had called a major flogging. What did that mean? What was the difference between a major and a minor flogging? Or an intermediate flogging, for that matter? That was the other word she had used. The only thing certain was that the major flogging was the worst of the three. But how bad would it be? How many lashes? And with what? A whip or a cat-o'-nine-tails? And when would it happen?

He gave a mental shrug to his shoulders and put the questions out of his mind. He would find out the answers soon enough. He would only increase his troubles by agonising about them now.

He closed his eyes and pictured her again as she had pronounced the sentence on him. "*You shall be flogged.*" He could swear that, as she spoke the words, there had been something like a caress in her eyes. It had almost been as though she regretted that she could not give the flogging herself.

He caught his breath sharply. God! What a lovely creature she was! He felt that he would not object to a flogging, major or not, if it was delivered by her own hand. In Cairo, some years before, he had taken part in a grand orgy of flagellation during which he himself whipped a very beautiful girl who was horsed over the backs of two other beautiful girls. After he had finished, they had tied him naked to a post and tantalised his penis and testicles with feathers and their finger-tips. When they brought him to the point of frenzy, they each took a whip and thrashed him. To his surprise, he found that it was not too unpleasant. It was shockingly painful, of course, but it was also exciting.

If he had to be flogged, he now thought, it was a very great pity that it could not be done by this breath-taking girl. He ought to have requested it! He grinned momentarily as he imagined the shock she would have had. But would she? There had been that curious look in her eyes...

He suddenly felt angry with himself. These were damn silly thoughts. She would assuredly have sent him to that labour camp. He had better stop thinking about her and get some sleep. He would need all his strength. He must put her out of his mind.

He turned over on his side, feeling the sweat rush out of his pores at the small exertion. He closed his eyes and willed himself to sleep.

At about the same time, the Princess Makasile was speaking into a telephone and putting certain wheels into motion. As a result, Saunders was rudely woken half an hour later. He was handcuffed again, chains were put back on to his feet, and he was taken along interminable passages in the prison until he found himself in surroundings that were considerably better furnished than those he had left. Along more passages, through more doors, he at last found himself in a cell which almost shone with whiteness and cleanliness. The door slammed shut behind him.

Still handcuffed and chained, he looked around his cell. It had a bed with a mattress on it, a chair, a table. He glanced at the table again, and widened his eyes. On it lay a short whip.

He lay down on the bed and gazed at the whip. Now, why should there be a whip in his cell? Was this what he was going to be flogged with? He sighed and stretched himself on the comfortable mattress. He glanced up at the cell window. He could not see the sun but he judged it to be about four o'clock in the afternoon. Another three or four hours and this terrible heat would have gone. He closed his eyes and went once more to sleep.

It was four hours later, and the heat had gone, when he was awakened again. He opened his eyes and found a good-looking girl standing beside his bed. The whip that had been lying on his table was now in her right hand. She was dressed in something like a sari of canary-yellow chiffon. This contrasted beautifully with her long dark hair. She looked extremely fetching. His eyes opened wide.

"You are to come with me," she said, in English. "Stand up."

He stared at her in amazement. "By all means," he said foolishly. "I'd love to come with you. But who are you? And where are we going?"

She slashed his chest with the whip. "You are to come, and without questions."

Pain burned through him, but he was too surprised to protest. He swung his chained ankles off the bed and stood up. The girl pointed to the cell door, which was now standing open. "Go," she said crisply. "Go quickly."

He walked out of the cell.

"To your left," she ordered. "Up the stairs."

He preceded her up a narrow spiral staircase. He realised to his great relief that his headache had at last left him, and that he had regained a good deal of his strength. He glanced over his shoulder at the girl.

"Who are you?" he asked again. "Where are we going?"

She did not answer. Nor did she slash him with her whip this time. It was probably because the staircase was too narrow for her to swing it properly. At the top there was a heavy wooden door, without a handle and without a keyhole. She climbed to the top step beside him and knocked sharply on the door with the handle of her whip. A beautiful perfume came from her body and made him dizzy with desire.

There was a noise of a bolt being slid. The door swung open.

She touched his arm with the whip-handle. He walked forward into a richly panelled, parquet-floored hall with several other doors. The door through which he had walked swung shut behind him. He heard the bolt being slid back into its place. He turned his head and gasped with surprise. Another girl stood there, dressed in the same sort of canary-yellow chiffon sari. And this one was equally pretty.

"Dear God," he murmured. "This is like the Arabian Nights. I must be dreaming." He glanced at the whip which had caused him the pain that was still burning in his chest. He knew that he was not dreaming. "Please tell me," he said to the girl who held the whip. "Where are we?"

"We are in the palace," she replied. She pointed to the floor. "And since this afternoon you have been in the palace prison underneath."

"But why?"

"You are to be flogged."

"*Here*, in the palace?"

"Yes."

A sudden hope leapt to his mind. "By you?"

She smiled. "No. But I shall use this—"she ran the lash of the whip through her fingers"—if you ask any more questions."

"But I *must* ask," he protested. "Who's going to flog me? And why here?"

She raised the whip and brought it down across his shoulders. "I warned you," she said sweetly. "Go into that room." She pointed to a facing door. "You're going to have a bath."

"A *bath!*" he echoed bewilderedly. "Dear God! I must be going crazy." He looked at the other girl. "Won't *you* tell me what this is all about?"

"She doesn't speak English," said the girl with the whip, and struck him again. "Do as I tell you. Go into that room."

He shrugged his burning shoulders and turned towards the door. "How is it that you do?" he asked suddenly.

"Do what?"

"Speak English."

"I was once in England. I learned it there."

"What were you doing in England?"

She raised the whip and struck him very hard across the shoulders. "Will you *stop* asking questions!" She suddenly felt ashamed of herself for being rather too cruel. "I accompanied my mistress," she said in a kindly tone that made him warm to her, despite the pain she had given him. "I stayed there for two years."

"Who is your mistress?" he asked irrepressibly.

She frowned. "Do you want me to whip you properly? I will, you know." She felt she had done her duty to decency in answering his last question but one. Now, however, he simply must be stopped. She raised her whip. "I've told you to go in that room. Do as I say." She forced herself to sound stern. The fact of the matter was that she was beginning to fall, as so many other women had done, under the spell of his attraction. She found herself wanting to put her arms around him, to kiss him, to make love to him.

She gave herself a mental shake. This would never do. Such thoughts would get her into a lot of trouble. She decided that she would have to be stern and sensible. To fortify this decision she raised her whip again and lashed him, not too heavily, across his shoulder-blades. "Go!" she repeated.

He looked at her, and shrugged his shoulders again. He went to the door and turned its handle with his manacled hands. Inside he found a large luxurious bathroom with a marble bath that was already filled with steaming hot water.

"I am going to remove your chains," said the girl, taking a key from somewhere beneath her chiffon. "But I warn you very seriously. Don't try to attack me. It would be terrible for you afterwards. And don't think of trying to get away. You could never manage it." She unlocked each of his handcuffs and knelt to remove the chains from his ankles. She stood up. "Now take your clothes off and get into that bath. Clean yourself properly."

He shook his head in total puzzlement. He said nothing. He took off his few clothes and stood naked in front of the girl. Her eyes flickered over his body appreciatively. "Get in and wash," she said sternly, as though she was angry with herself for admiring his naked manliness.

He stepped into the bath. Accustomed as he was to salt-water showers on board the tanker, with the necessarily rough salt-water soap, it was like paradise to be able to lie back in sweetly perfumed hot water and pick up the cake of equally sweetly perfumed soap. He began to forget that he still had a flogging in front of him. He soaped his arms and shoulders luxuriously.

"Don't take too long," said the girl. She leaned against the wall, her whip hanging down beside her.

Now in bubbling high spirits, he grinned at her. "Are you going to do my back?"

She moved her whip slightly. "I'll do it with this if you don't obey me."

He grinned again. "Come on, now. Do tell me. Who are you?" He realised that it would be difficult now for her to use her whip on him. "Please tell me."

"I am the servant of—" she paused a second "—a high personage in the palace."

He nodded sagely. "I see. And has this high personage anything to do with my punishment?"

"Yes."

"What, may I ask?"

She looked at him, her head a little on one side. "There's no reason really why you shouldn't know. You are going to be flogged by this personage."

He stopped soaping himself and stared at her. "Why?"

She shook her head. "No more questions now. You will soon see for yourself. Come on, hurry up."

When he had finished his bath and stepped out on to the tiled floor, she handed him a large white towel. He dried himself and reached for his trousers. "No," she said. "From now on you will remain without clothes. Come along." She picked up his handcuffs and chains, and stood aside for him to go through the door. In the hall she pointed to another door. "In there," she ordered.

He put his hand on the door-handle and turned it. He gave the door an ordinary push. It hardly moved. He pushed harder. It swung open, slowly and heavily. He saw that it was extremely thick, with several inches of heavy quilted padding on its inside. He frowned at this thoughtfully for a second—and then shivered as he realised that it was clearly a form of sound-proofing. And so the room was a punishment room.

But the punishments delivered here must be severe indeed, he thought. Why, otherwise, should this door be so thickly sound proofed?

The interior was dark. He stood still, undecided what to do.

She lashed him, quite lightly, across his buttocks. "What are you waiting for? Go *in!*"

He stepped over the threshold. He sniffed. Then he inhaled deeply. The room had a deliciously musky smell. He came to a halt again.

She followed him in and reached for the light switches.

His mouth fell open in horrified shock as the room was revealed to him. "Oh *no!*" His voice was a hoarse whisper. "Oh, Jesus Christ!"

The room was a well-equipped whipping room. In one way, it resembled a padded-cell in a lunatic asylum, for all its walls, as well as the inside of the door, were covered with thick quilted padding. But the resemblance ended there, for padded cells are usually small—and this room was quite large, about thirty feet by twenty; padded cells have only their walls covered, and they have a window of some sort: the ceiling of this room was also padded and there was no window. It was ventilated by a system of central air-conditioning.

"Go in!" she repeated, lashing him across the buttocks again, harder this time. "Don't just stand there."

He walked slowly to the centre of the room, looking about him incredulously.

In the middle of the floor was an obvious whipping post—but unlike what he had imagined a whipping post would be. He had never seen one but he had had the idea that they were usually triangular, the victim's wrists being tied to the apex, his ankles to the feet. This one was like a ladder standing perpendicularly between the floor and the ceiling. Its sides were wider apart than a ladder's would be—in order, it was clear, to enable the victim to stand within the two sides, and it had but three rungs. One was on a level with where the average victim's knees would be, the second on a level with his stomach, the third on a level with his neck. As he stared dumbly at this contraption, he noticed that the rungs were not fixed: their ends were set in slots in the sides of the "ladder," with screw fastenings; this movability clearly enabled them to be set at the height required for each individual victim. From each of the three rungs hung strong leather straps with heavy metal buckles. About eight feet above the floor, a shining steel manacle dangled from each side of the "ladder," and to the foot of each side there was attached a similarly shining leg-iron.

She lashed his buttocks again. "Stand in between the posts," she ordered. "You must be tied up. Hurry!"

He obeyed her, his heart sinking with fearful despair. He continued to inspect the room.

It had not much furniture. There were four three-legged stools with comfortable-looking seats of padded leather. There were a couple of small tables with silver boxes, cigarette lighters and ashtrays on them, a glass-fronted cabinet with bottles and glasses showing through, and something like a clothes rack on four small rubber wheels.

It was this that caught his principal attention, and made his heart thump painfully with terror. It was a rack not for clothes but for whips and other implements of flagellation. They hung from hooks, a foot apart from one another.

"Put your hands above your head," she said, accompanying the order with the now-expected lash across his buttocks. "High." She moved a stool beside the whipping-post and stood up on it.

He stretched his hands up to the cold steel manacles and felt his wrists being imprisoned. He did not take his eyes away from the whips.

The one nearest to him was about five feet in length. It began, at its handle end, with the thickness of a man's thumb and tapered down to something of the thickness of a pencil. At its tip there was a small knotted thong. Next to this long whip there was a much shorter one, no more than two-and-a-half feet long, but of the same thickness. Next there was a cat-o'-nine-tails that made him catch his breath. It had a handle of what looked like lacquered wood into which were set a large number of jewels. From the rich handle hung the lashes, nine of them. These were made of strips of square-edged leather, about two feet in length, with small lead weights, of the size of an aspirin, attached to the tip of each.

The girl stepped down from the stool. "Open your legs," she ordered. She did not lash him this time. She had put down her whip before she had begun to fasten his wrists. "Put your ankles against the sides of the post."

"And this is supposed to be the twentieth century," he said, as he obeyed. "Jesus Christ!"

She made no comment. She knelt and secured his ankles.

Next to the cat-o'-nine-tails, he saw, there was a terrible whip made of dozens of lengths of fine wire. He regarded it with awe. That sort of whip, he thought, was a weapon that could very easily kill...

"Now stand closely against the middle bar," she said. She strapped him by his stomach tightly to the second rung. She secured his knees to the first rung in the same way. She stood erect and unscrewed the top rung. She moved it into position. "Put your chin over this," she said, giving his head a push to help him to understand. He felt the strap being passed round his neck and drawn tight.

A feeling of claustrophobia swept over him. He pulled on all his bonds. He tried to wriggle his body. He could make no movement. He was utterly helpless. His senses began to swim.

The girl looked at him kindly. By some instinct

she understood what he was suffering. She put a hand on his shoulder. "Relax," she said quietly. "Don't fight this. It will make everything worse for you."

He sensed that she was right. He forced himself to relax. It was a tremendous effort, but at last he won back his self control, and the feeling of the insanity-bringing claustrophobia left him. He went back to regarding the whips in front of him.

Next to the whip of wire there was a long, slinky riding switch. It could obviously give great pain but in comparison with the other whips it looked like the toy of a child. Next to it hung an instrument that looked like a wide, thick belt. It was made of black rubber, and it was cut down the centre for the length of a foot and a half.

The only other instrument that hung from the rack made him frown in puzzlement. It was a miniature cat-o'-nine-tails, almost an exact replica of the other one. Its handle, equally richly encrusted with jewels, was about six inches long; its nine lashes were about twelve inches long. He wondered what such a miniature could be used for. A thought came to his mind for a second, chilled him to ice, and was thrust away at once.

The girl saw what he was looking at, noticed his involuntary start of terror, and wondered whether to tell him what it was used for. She decided against it. He would learn soon enough.

He now began to wonder why he had been so idiotic as to obey her in everything she had ordered him to do. Couldn't he have overpowered her—and made a dash for it? But how?—without clothes. He had noticed the other girl taking his clothes away from the bathroom as he had crossed the hall. He would never have been able to find them. But even if he had, how could he have made his way out of the building? No, after all, he had not been idiotic in obeying the girl. He had been idiotic the night before in the Palace Hotel. He had been idiotic in leaving his ship, in coming ashore at all, in taking no notice of his captain. He sighed. "One lives and learns," he murmured to himself.

"What did you say?" asked the girl, sitting very gracefully down on one of the stools in front of him.

"Nothing much," he said. "But you can tell me something, if you will."

"Perhaps."

"What is a major flogging? And what's an intermediate one and a minor one?"

"A major flogging carries a hundred lashes. An intermediate, fifty. A minor twenty-five."

"A *hundred!* Christ!" He stared at her with wide-open eyes.

She smiled sympathetically. "Here, it could be more."

"What do you mean?"

"I mean that the major, intermediate and minor limits are really for the floggings that are given in the prison itself. Here, in the palace, it rather depends."

"Depends? For Christ's sake, on what?"

"On how the—the person who is going to give the flogging feels. That's why it could be more than a hundred." She looked at him with some compassion. "On the other hand, it could be fewer—if she feels sorry for you—or if she's not feeling over-energetic."

"That's nice to know," he said sarcastically, and suddenly stopped. He stared wide-eyed at her. "*She!* Did you say *she?*"

A hand flew to her mouth. She reddened. "My God, I did, didn't I?" She moved her position as though to throw off a feeling of some sort of guilt. "Oh well, it doesn't really matter now. She'll be here soon. But do me a favour, will you?" She looked up at him appealingly. "Let it be a surprise, when she comes."

"That won't be difficult," he said grimly.

"No," she answered uncomfortably. "I mean something else. Please don't let her see that you knew you were going to be flogged by a woman. Pretend to be surprised, will you? I'm not supposed to have told you."

He tried to nod his head, but found he could not move it more than a quarter of an inch. He flickered his eyelids instead. "All right. But tell me a bit more."

"No, no more. I've said too much already."

"Oh, come on. It can't do any harm now. Who is this woman?"

She sighed. "Oh well. You'll know in a few moments anyway. She is the Princess Makasile."

"Who on earth is that?"

"The King's daughter."

"But why? What reason—"

She stood up abruptly and turned her back on him. "No more questions now," she said firmly. "Just wait and see."

His thoughts were racing. The Princess Makasile. He was going to be flogged by a royal princess. He had been beginning to ask what reason she could have for wanting to flog him, but he realised now that the question was naive and stupid. The memory of his flagellation orgy in Cairo came back to him. People flogged and flagellated for one reason only: it gave them pleasure. And so the Princess Makasile was obviously a flagellating sadist. But what would she look like? How old was she? If she was at all young and attractive, a flogging at her hands, might conceivably have some possibility of excitement. But if she was an old shrewish-looking hag—and this, after all, was the more likely—there would be no such excitement.

"Do tell me," he pleaded. "What does she look like? Is she young?"

"Ssshh!" she whispered suddenly, her eyes going to the door behind him.

He watched her make a deep curtsy to someone who obviously had just entered the room. She said something in her own language.

"Continue to speak in English," said a low well-modulated voice that he was sure he recognised. His heart leapt. But it was too good to be true! And yet he could swear that it was the voice of his judge—and she had been addressed as Highness... Oh God! If only it were true! He waited in an agony of suspense for whoever it was to come into the line of his vision. When she did so, he gave such a gasp of relieved astonishment that the girl in the yellow chiffon sari threw him a glance of gratitude.

The Princess smiled. "Yes, I thought you'd be surprised, my friend."

He was unable to reply. He gazed at her with rapturous admiration. She was dressed in Persian-type pyjamas of sheer, transparent black chiffon. Under these she wore nothing else. Her breasts, her stomach, the dark hairs of her genitals were all tantalisingly half-visible. On her feet she wore court-style shoes with very high pointed heels.

She stood regarding him with interest. His body was muscular and well-formed. She was going to enjoy this flogging. It was a long time since she had been able to flog anyone so attractive. She wondered how he would take it. Would he be very brave and tough and manly—and refuse to scream? Or *try* to refuse to scream, rather? Sooner or later she would make him scream, of course. No one had ever been able to keep silent under the whip with the wire lashes, however brave they might have been under the others.

She came up close to him. She put a hand to his body. It was cool and soft. Her perfume came to his nose and made him ache with desire for her.

"Have you ever been tied up like this before?" she murmured.

"No," he said, "never."

She ran her hand over his shoulders. "You can't move, you handsome person, can you?" She felt the muscles of his arms. "You're more helpless than you've ever believed possible, aren't you?" There was a caress in her voice, but it was a caress of cruelty.

"Yes," he said. "I'm helpless, all right."

She ran her hand over his stomach. She felt his muscles tightening under her touch.

He was in a turmoil of conflicting emotions. Her nearness, her near-nakedness, her perfume, her cool hand playing over his flesh—all these things gave him an intense pleasure. The cruelty in her voice, however, brought back the thought of the flogging that was to come. And yet... he didn't really mind... since it was she who was going to flog him. In Cairo, he forced himself to remember, it had been quite pleasant being whipped by those girls. But—he also remembered—in Cairo the girls had not used the sort of whips that were here in front of his eyes. And he had not been made quite so immovably helpless. This whipping was obviously going to be very terrible. He was going to suffer a lot. He had better stop thinking that it would be exciting—simply because the whipper was the loveliest woman he had ever seen in his life. That was utter nonsense.

He gazed at her as she continued to touch his body. Oh God! She was quite unbelievably lovely. There surely had never been such a woman before.

His thoughts turned another somersault. He went back to thinking that the whipping—so long as she herself gave it—might not be so terrible after all...

Her hand had begun to play with the hairs above his penis. He wondered whether there was the slightest chance that she might actually take hold of the thing itself. On this thought, the penis erected suddenly and magnificently.

"Oho!" she said, and took it in her hand. "This is not supposed to happen yet."

A sweet tingle filled his loins. "Yet?" he said, enquiringly. The word seemed to have a possible promise. "Why do you say 'yet'?"

She laughed. "Oh, because—" She stopped suddenly. "Never you mind. Wait and see."

She let go of his penis and walked to the hanging whips. She took hold of the longest and lifted it from its hook. She gazed at it reflectively for a moment or two. She raised it above her head and struck at the floor. It gave a sharp hiss as its lash cut through the air, and then a loud crack as it hit.

He winced at the two sounds. *That* was going to happen to his body! He must have been quite out of his mind to think that it might not be too terrible.

She looked at his body again. She was thinking that it was the last time she would ever see it unmarked, unlacerated. The thought made her heart bump with excitement. She began to feel more sexy than ever.

She came back to him, the long whip in her right hand. She took hold of his penis again with her left. "Which shall I start with?" she murmured, looking deeply into his eyes, recognising the fear, and relishing it. She agitated his penis lightly and felt it grow larger and harder in her palm. "You're very virile, aren't you?" she said. "With a flogging in front of you, I'm surprised that you can go so stiff as this. I should have thought you would be far too frightened."

"I am frightened," he said candidly. "But what you're doing at the moment is not frightening. It's wonderful."

She squeezed the penis. "Suppose I were to flog this a little, too? Would it still be wonderful?"

"You surely can't be serious?" But he was not at all sure. Her tone was certainly light enough, but nevertheless there was some undercurrent of seriousness in it. It was not completely impossible that such a horror was in her mind.

"Why not?" She looked at him in surprise. "Why shouldn't I flog your—your john-thomas? Isn't that what you call it in your country?"

"Yes, among other things," he said, feeling more than ever afraid. He pulled again on his bonds. It was a reflex, involuntary pulling, without hope of reward, for he had by now been standing in his helpless trussed-up position for long enough to be fully aware of the meaning of immobility.

"So why shouldn't I flog it?"

"But you— I mean, you surely don't flog people *there!*"

Her eyes widened. She looked at him quizzically, the merriment dancing in her expression. "Salome," she said, without turning her head.

The girl who had tied him up came silently to her mistress.

"Highness?" She stood with her eyes respectfully downcast.

"Bring me the small cat-o'-nine-tails."

His heart sank with sickening suddenness. Unconsciously he had been trying not to think of that small cat-o'-nine-tails, for some instinct had already suggested to him that it might conceivably be used for such a purpose. The thought had been so shocking, however, that he had put it out of his mind and, subconsciously, had been doing his best to keep it out.

The girl bowed her head and went to the whips rack. She took down the small nine-lashed instrument. She brought it to her mistress.

The Princess Makasile handed her the long whip. "Hold that a moment." She took the cat-o'-nine-tails in her right hand. She looked into his eyes again. "You think that we don't flog people's john-thomases, do you? That's very curious. I know that it's not done much in England but I find it curious that you haven't learned that it's done a lot in the Middle East." She stepped a pace away from him. She measured her distance.

"Please no!" he gasped, seeing what was about to happen. "For God's sake, please don't to that!"

She swung the cat-o'-nine-tails sideways. The tails gave a quick swooshing noise—and then struck his erected penis.

A shaft of poignant pain stabbed through his loins, searingly, agonisingly. He felt dizzy with it for a moment.

"That wasn't so bad, was it?" he heard her say again. "Many men find that it is pleasant. Old men, particularly." She struck him again.

"I'm not an old man," he said, through gritted teeth, squirming in his bonds as the pain ravaged him. "That's—probably why—I don't—find—it at all pleasant." He felt he had to make some form of conversation or else he might start screaming.

She seemed to sense what he was thinking. "Scream, if it helps you," she said, delivering the third lash. "As you've seen, this room is nicely sound proofed. Nobody but us two will hear you—and we like to listen to a man screaming." She swung the whip again. "Salome, in fact, adores it." *Lash!* "That's one of three things she learned when she was in England with me." *Lash!* "She learned to speak English. She learned to whip the English. And she learned to adore the sound of an Englishman screaming."

She delivered another lash and gave the cat-o'-nine-tails back to Salome. She took the long whip again into her hand. "That is just a little taste of the thing that Middle Eastern women like to do to john-thomases." She paused, and frowned. His eyes were shut. He seemed to have fainted. She put her free hand to the now soft penis and gave it a pull. "Hey!" she said sharply. "Are you asleep or something?"

He opened his eyes, squinted, focussed his gaze. "No," he said quietly. "Not asleep. Just in dreadful pain. That was a terrible thing to do."

She fondled the lacerated penis. Some drops of blood had been brought on its knob, on its column, and on the testicle-bag. She ran her index finger lightly up and down the central nerve.

The penis was so sore after its ill-treatment that her fingers gave him a good deal of discomfort, but, beneath the discomfort, and amid the pain which still burned through him, a small tingling sensation of sexual pleasure began to hover round his genital area. Under the delicious, if painful, play of her fingers, he felt the stiffness return slowly but surely to his penis.

He wished he could move his head enough to look down and make sure—because it did not seem possible that any penis could ever have another erection after such a flogging. And yet, astonishing though it was, his own erection was steadily mounting. Though he could not see it, there was no ambiguity about the sensation that was being caused by her fingers. He was quite sure. He was already fully re-erected.

She gave the penis a slap. "Congratulations! That was really quite quick." She stood back. "And now comes the first part of your proper flogging. Fifty strokes with this." She held the handle to his lips. "Kiss it."

He made a kissing movement with his lips.

She chuckled. "That's English, you know."

"What is?" He swallowed with difficulty. His mouth was very dry.

"The practice of making the victim kiss whatever he is going to be beaten with. Didn't you know?"

"Yes, vaguely," he said, swallowing again. "Look, before you start, could you give me something to drink?"

She pursed her lips. "For strength, hmm?"

He began the motion of shaking his head, and stopped at once. He determined to remember not to make these involuntary movements. The fact that they were impossible made it worse for him. And he did not want any return of that earlier claustrophobia. "No. Just water, please. My throat is like a desert."

She nodded slightly. "Water, Salome."

He watched the girl open the glass-fronted cabinet and pour water from a carafe into a tall glass. She brought it to him and, tip-toeing, put it to his lips. He swallowed with difficulty but with gratitude.

"You can also have a stronger drink if you like," said Makasile, "Whisky?"

He realised that he would now like it very much "Yes, please."

"A large whisky, Salome," said Makasile. She swished the whip around her as she waited. She did not feel in any hurry.

The whisky burned pleasantly and made him feel momentarily a lot better.

"Your john-thomas is still enormous," said Makasile. "It does you credit." She was thinking of the thing that she was going to do to it, after these fifty strokes of her whip. Her heart began to beat faster at the mental picture. She glanced up at him. "You know, I'm going to be kind to you. I'm going to let Salome play with it while I flog you." She turned to the girl. "You'd like that, wouldn't you?"

"Yes, please, Highness," said Salome simply.

"But, be careful," said Makasile sternly. "Whatever you do, you must not let him come."

"That is understood, Highness."

"Though I doubt," added Makasile grimly, "whether anyone could *possibly* come while he's being flogged as I'm now going to flog him."

She walked out of the range of his vision and took up her position behind the whipping post. She measured the distance with her eye, flexed the muscles of her right arm—the whip dangling floorwards as she did so—and drew a long, deep, excitement-filled, tremulous breath.

In the meantime, Salome quickly picked up one of the three-legged stools and put it down in front of the whipping post. She sat down on it, hutched it a little nearer to him, moved her position so that she was sitting sideways—and took his penis in her hands. She caught her breath sharply as she did so.

He heard the catch of her breath, and realised that she was indeed going to enjoy playing with him. He reflected ruefully that he could have had a very wonderful time with her the previous night, if he had only accosted her instead of the wife of an important Shaikh.

In the middle of this thought, five things happened—almost simultaneously.

He heard the swish of the whip as it descended for the first stroke...

He tensed every muscle in his body, and held his breath...

He felt his penis being engulfed by what could only be Salome's lips and mouth...

The whip cut across the exact centre of his buttocks...

He felt a white-hot barb of pain—and an almost instantaneous thrill of pleasure.

He let out his breath with a rush. Jesus Christ! he thought fervidly. It was *not* so bad! It was like that time in Cairo—thrilling and pleasant. But this was even better. In Cairo there had not been a girl putting his penis in her mouth. This was going to be rather nice...

He heard the swish of the whip again. He changed his mind at once as the lash this time struck him across his shoulder blades, and there was now only pain, pain, pain! No! This was not going to be nice, after all. Not unless she would concentrate on his bottom, and leave his back alone. He could stand it on his bottom. He could even get a thrill out of it. But his back, no! That was just plain bloody murder.

The third lash struck his buttocks again, made his senses reel with agony, and again—almost at once—brought the thrill of pleasure...

Makasile thrashed slowly and deliberately. Her pleasure came from striking carefully at a previously selected part of the body, and savouring to the fullest extent the quiver of agony that ran through the protesting muscles. Her aim was remarkably good. But then it ought to be: she gave herself a good deal of practice. The only trouble, she was now thinking, was that so few of the victims were attractive enough to stimulate her appetites to anything other than pure flagellation.

This man, however, was different. He was very attractive indeed. She was looking forward very much to satisfying a certain other appetite. And she would do this as soon as she had delivered the first fifty.

Salome sat with the still mightily-erected penis in her mouth, her fingers playing lightly and deliciously with the skin of his testicle bag. She was enjoying herself very much. It was not often that her mistress allowed her to do this to a victim. It happened, she realised, only when the Princess was herself attracted by the victim. But when it did happen, she enjoyed it—as much as she was allowed to enjoy it. She found it very pleasant to lick and suck and bite the penis of a victim. If she were only permitted to go as far as her mistress always went, when she put a penis into her mouth, things would be a great deal better. But then, she thought, as she gave a little pinch with her fingernails to the testicle bag, you couldn't have everything—and being a servant of the Princess Makasile had some very great advantages. She wondered whether she would be allowed to do some whipping too. It seemed very likely, for it was almost certain that the Princess was going to indulge her own very private pleasure on this victim. And when she did that, she always required someone else to do some whipping.

Salome pulled back her head and looked up at Saunders.

His face was twisted into a grimace of affliction as the lashes struck him alternately across his back and his bottom. Each time the whip struck his bottom he received the thrill of pleasure; each time it struck his back or shoulders the thrill of pleasure was plucked away as though it had never existed. But all the time there was the sweet sensation in his penis and testicles.

"Please," he begged, speaking through clenched jaws. "Don't—stop—doing—that!"

Salome nodded quickly and contritely, and put her mouth once more to his penis. Something of its stiffness had gone away in the few seconds in which she had been looking up at him, but now, under the play of her tongue and teeth, it came back with full potential.

The Princess Makasile was beginning to feel tired. She found it curious. She had not delivered more than thirty-five lashes. Why should she feel tired—she who could deliver three hundred if need be? She analysed herself coolly, as she went on lashing. There was only one possible reason. She had already sublimated her sadism over this man with this short thrashing. Now she needed fulfilment.

At once, she let her arm fall. Well and good. If that was what had happened—and it seemed pretty certain that it was—there was only one thing to do: to go on to the next stage and satisfy herself to the full. It would mean that he would get off very lightly, but that didn't matter. He hadn't really been brought here for punishment. But he would have to be flogged more thoroughly another day.

She sat down on a nearby stool. Yes, she was very tired. Her heart was beating heavily, almost painfully. Her limbs were full of that aching sweetness that comes to those who flagellate a helpless victim. Her loins were on fire. Her vagina was drenched in preliminary juices which had gathered under the stimulation of the sadistic pleasure.

Salome realised, with a start, that the flogging had come to an end. She smiled inwardly. Her mistress must be very impatient for the next stage in the proceedings. She removed her mouth, stood up, and murmured: "You're very lucky!"

She went to the cabinet and poured some whisky into a glass. She took it to her mistress, bowed, and proffered it silently.

Equally silently, Makasile took the glass and drained it. Then she said: "Give him some, too."

As the burning liquor went down his throat for the second time, he said: "What's going to happen now?"

"Something rather nice," said Salome, very quietly. "You'll like it."

"What is it?"

"Sssshh."

"No, do tell me."

"No. Ssshh! Finish the glass."

He gulped down the last drops of the drink, and wondered what she could have meant. What pleasant thing could possibly be coming to him now?

Makasile stood up. She came back into his line of vision. She was still holding the whip. His spirits dropped as he saw it. She saw the gloom gather in his eyes, and laughed. "No, no more. At least for the time being. Here, Salome, take it."

The girl took the whip and put it back on its hook. It was not clear whether it would be needed again. If not, she would have to remember to take it away to wash it. A lot of blood had congealed on its lash-end.

Makasile sat down on the stool that Salome had been sitting on. She put her hands to his penis again. "You are probably going to enjoy the next part," she said, looking up at him.

"What are you going to do?"

She hesitated. She always felt a touch of embarrassment at admitting her perversion. She did not, of course, regard her pleasure in flagellation as a perversion of any sort, but this other pleasure of hers was—well, it was just a little unusual. "I'm going, first of all, to do what Salome did."

His heart gave a leap. The very idea that such a lovely creature could put his penis into her mouth was enough to make his senses swim. "Yes?" he said, enquiringly. She had said "first of all." There must be something else.

"And I'm going to give you an orgasm."

Dear God! An orgasm! What absolute heaven! But why should she? For what possible reason? "Good heavens!" he said cautiously.

"You're wondering why."

"Yes. Frankly, I am." His penis in her hands was getting larger and harder than ever.

"And Salome will be whipping you while I'm bringing you to the orgasm."

"Oh."

"Don't you wonder about that? Doesn't that make you curious too?"

He sighed. "Not really. If you're going to give me an orgasm—well, that's enough for me." His eyes suddenly twinkled with amusement. "It might be dangerous to ask too many questions."

She smiled back at him. "I'll tell you anyway." Her momentary embarrassment had disappeared. "Salome's job will be to give you just enough pain to stop you coming too quickly. But when I'm ready for you to come, I shall let you come—and then she'll *really* whip you." She paused. "That's something you will enjoy, though. I can promise you that. You may not understand it, but you can believe me."

"I believe you," he said, thinking again of Cairo, and of the thrill he had just experienced when her own whip had struck his buttocks. "And—and you're going to bring me—with your *mouth?*" It was really to good to be true.

"I am," she said. "And something else." The time had come to tell him of her perversion. Some of her embarrassment returned.

"Yes?"

"I'm going to drink your juices." There, it was out.

He was silent, wondering whether to believe his ears. If they were reliable, she had said that she was going to drink his sperm—which meant that she would keep his penis in her mouth right up to, and beyond, the last moments—which in turn meant that he would be able to do what amounted to making love to her mouth, thrusting his ejaculating weapon far inside....

Good heavens! He was most certainly going to enjoy the next part!

It came to him suddenly that he would not be able to do any thrusting, after all. His loins were strapped so tightly to the centre rung of the whipping post, and his knees so securely to the lower rung, that even the minutest thrust was out of the question. Mentally, he shrugged his shoulders. It really did not matter. In a way, it might even be more pleasant—her having all the initiative.

He realised that there had been a silence for too long. He had better say something in reply to her last statement.

"The only thing I can say," he said quietly, "is that I'm speechless—but speechless with excitement."

"Good," she said. "Then let's start the mad game."

There were times when she wondered whether perhaps she was indeed a little mad—at any rate over this perversion. It had begun when she was at her finishing school. A lover had persuaded her to give him the thrill of having his penis sucked by her mouth, licked by her tongue, bitten by her teeth. He had become so excited that, suddenly, unexpectedly and violently, he had shot his juices far into her mouth. Convulsively, she had swallowed them.

And she had received the greatest thrill of her life.

After that, she began to lose interest in ordinary copulation. What she wanted more than anything else was to undo the trousers of her lover, kneel in front of him, and bring him to an orgasm—and slowly swallow the juices.

The only thing that she disliked was that her lover, and other men who followed him, took so much delight in her private form of love-making that the orgasm arrived almost before she felt that she had started to enjoy herself.

Later, when she was initiated to the delights of flagellation, she found that pain could be used to hold the orgasm in check for as long as she wanted. All that was necessary was an assistant. While she herself indulged her perversion, her assistant would deliver, under her direction, just the right amount of pain. And so she could indulge herself as much, and for as long, as her heart desired.

"Use the riding switch," she said now to Salone. "He's already so cut up, it will give quite enough pain. But watch my hand carefully."

"But naturally, Highness." And Salome ran to the whips rack.

Makasile moved her position on her stool, made herself comfortable, and cupped his penis in both her hands. It was still an angry red from her earlier flogging with the small cat-o'-nine-tails. She gazed at its knob with hungry eyes. She lowered her head, put out the tip of her tongue and licked the tiny slit. She gave a great shuddering sigh, opened her mouth and engulfed as much as possible. She felt the quiver of pleasure run through his loins. She lifted a hand for a moment. It had two fingers extended.

Salome, having taken the switch from the whips rack and put herself into position, nodded as she saw the two fingers. She began to lash the tender part of the legs between the lower part of his buttocks and the back of his knees. One finger extended would have shown that less pain was required, and she would have thrashed the buttocks themselves. Three fingers called for a greater degree of pain—across the shoulders. And four fingers meant that she was free to whip wherever and however she wanted: the orgasm was arriving—and no amount of pain could stop it. That was the moment that Salome loved. She was able to plunge her own self at last into the sea of sadistic satisfaction. But that would not come for some time. Her mistress usually held it back for at least twenty minutes.

Apart from the ultimate joy of drinking the juices, Makasile's pleasure came largely from this very fact of being able to hold an orgasm tremblingly in check for so long: to entice it forward, to drive it away, to entice it again...

Her course of action was this. The man had usually become extremely excited—as a result of the preliminaries and of the thought of what was going to happen to him—even before she put her lips to his penis. Playing deliciously on his central nerve with her tongue, she was therefore able to stimulate his reactions sufficiently to bring the orgiastic ejaculation to a point just beneath its explosive fulfilment. And then she would raise her hand—with one or two fingers outstretched. The orgasm would recede under the pain. She would wait for it to subside sufficiently for safety— and then would start again with her tongue. The next time she raised her hand, it might be necessary to show three fingers: the orgasm this time could well be behaving obstinately. But the pain of the lashing across the shoulders never failed—at *this* point, at any rate—to drive it away again. And then she would start once more. When, finally, she felt she had had enough of this peculiar pleasure (or on the rare occasions when she failed to hold the orgasm in check), she would let it come freely. And when she felt its actual arrival she would hold up four fingers. And Salome would begin to flog like a demon possessed.

The pain at this time was very great for the man, but, once his orgasm had actually begun, no amount of pain could drive it away. Pain, in fact, had the opposite effect: it increased the duration of the orgasm, it increased the quantity of juices produced—and so it pleased Makasile the more. The fact that the man also felt a great deal more pleasure himself was an incidental matter. She would not have been concerned if he had not; but she was basically a kind-hearted creature (as are nearly all women who indulge in sexual flagellation) and so she was happy that his own pains and agonies changed at the last moment into something he could enjoy.

At this moment, however, Saunders was not enjoying anything. He had been excessively randy when he felt Makasile kissing the slit of his penis—his randiness having been partly initiated by the mouth and tongue of Salome during his flogging—and he had felt that he would come at any second. At the back of his mind there had been a regret that, if he did, everything would be over far too quickly—but there was nothing he could do about it. He did not know that Makasile had already sensed this situation and had taken steps, with her two outstretched fingers, to rectify it. What he did know was that the lovely but sadistic Salome was hurting him very much with the riding switch. If only she would *not* hit him on that particular part of his legs! If only she would aim at his bottom... He suddenly remembered the words of Makasile: "Salome's job will be to give you just enough pain to stop you coming too quickly." She was doing that very thing at this moment. It must be by some pre-arrangement between them. And it was certainly succeeding in its purpose. His orgasm had receded considerably. He found himself, despite the pain, approving of the procedure: at least he would not finish everything too quickly. He remembered the other words of Makasile: "But when I'm ready for you to come, I shall let you come—and then she'll *really* whip you." He realised that this was no idle threat, but he felt no fear. His experiences in Cairo had taught him that a man can stand—can enjoy, in fact—any amount of pain at the moment of orgasm. It was something that Makasile had learned, too, for she had said: "That's something you will enjoy, though. I can promise you that. You may not understand it, but you can believe me." Yes, he was quite ready to believe her.

And so he stood there, immobile, helpless, being given great pain on one side of his body and tremendous ecstatic excitement on the other.

He began to wonder what was going to happen to him after all this was over. Presumably he would be released. He had been charged with an offence; he had had a trial—a travesty, of course, but nevertheless something that in Gubadan would pass for a trial. He had been sentenced to a certain punishment. And he was now receiving part of the punishment. He was also receiving other things which he had not expected. This soixante-neuf, or gamaroosh, or whatever it was called... But he was feeling very worried.

He tried to analyse his worry, as the switch continued to cut into his legs and as the tongue played with his penis. He was in a condition of neutrality, as far as his sexual excitement was concerned: the pain and the pleasure were just balancing each other. So he was able to think of other things.

Would he be set free when it was all over? Or would it be thought that he knew too much? He knew, after all, that the King's daughter had a number of rather shocking perversions... And foreign newspapers would pay a lot of money for the details! If he were to be set free, he would of course be asked to promise to keep his mouth shut. But would she risk that he would keep his word?

He asked himself what he would do if he were in her shoes.

With a shiver of fear, he had to admit that he would not risk such a thing.

So that might mean that he would not be released at all...

He shivered again. This was altogether terrible. Was he to be a captive? A member of a sort of male harem? A permanent whipping-boy?

At this moment of his thoughts, Makasile raised her hand and showed one finger.

Salome at once changed her aim and began to lash his buttocks.

After a few lashes he began to feel an upsurge of thrilling pleasure. His orgasm came back to life. It began to creep upwards—slowly at first—and then madly, tumultuously, irrepressibly... He totally forgot his anxieties.

Makasile raised three fingers. His fulfilment was too near.

The switch cut into his shoulder—blades. The thrilling pain changed to an agony that deadened all sexual pleasure. His orgasm receded again.

He returned to his anxieties. If they wanted to hold him captive, could they do it? Could such things be done in the twentieth century? Surely not.

In a moment he sadly decided that they could very probably be done—in such a Kingdom as Gubadan.

But, if so, he would surely be able to escape. They couldn't keep him in such close confinement as all that. The best thing for him to do, he told himself, was to stop anguishing about all these things. Let them take their course. And after all, he wasn't in such a bad situation now, was he? The loveliest girl he had ever seen in his life sitting on a stool in front of him with his penis in her mouth, maddening him with her tongue. And an extremely pretty girl as her assistant who seemed to like to do the same thing. Why, in the name of heaven, should he *want* to be set free? There was a dreadful amount of pain, it was true. But some of the pain was exciting. And he could quite easily stand the rest. Yes... yes. Perhaps he shouldn't really want to be released. At any rate, not yet.

This last thought had been caused, without his knowledge, by the fact that Salome had seen another signal of her mistress's hand. One finger. She had transferred her aim back to the lacerated, bleeding buttocks—and this, despite the laceration and the blood, had restored his pleasure almost without his realising it.

The sensation that he now began to experience once more was of an unbelievable sweetness. It was as though his sexual nerves had been separated and stretched on to the wood of a perfect violin. And the bow that was playing the violin was not made of the usual soft—hard hairy strands: it was compounded of a material as soft as down, as slippery as the moist inside of a woman's vagina... And it gave a sensation as sensitive, on the one hand, as the waters of Niagara Falls thundering downwards to the maelstrom below. And over il all there crashed wave after wave of sweetness...

He felt the irrepressible upsurge of his orgasm. He became tense all over—tenser even than the stretched strings of a violin. He began to hold his breath in pure rapture. He almost began to long for more pain...

Makasile felt the tenseness. She realised the imminent danger. She raised three fingers at once.

Salome changed aim like lightning. She lashed at the shoulders again.

It was too late. Pain could no longer have any restraint.

The orgasm mounted relentlessly... higher... stronger... nearer and nearer to its zenith.

Makasile realised suddenly that she had lost control. She immediately held up all her four fingers. She prepared herself, breathlessly, to take her fulfilment.

Salome came, as it were, to demoniac life. It was as though she had suddenly become electrified. She opened her legs wider and began to hit, hit, hit... She no longer timed her lashes to a steady, slow, deliberate rhythm. She lashed, forehandedly and backhandedly, as fast as she could, with all the strength of her arm, at his shoulders, bottom, calves, everywhere... And she felt her own orgasm leap forward. With each lash that she delivered, it gave a luscious little jump.

Saunders felt himself being somehow lifted out of himself. Never in his life had he experienced such an intoxicating bliss. The pain and the pleasure commingled like two unearthly perfumes. His senses swam. He let them swim. He was content to lest himself ride on the crest of this unbelievable mingling of sensations.

Makasile no longer tried to hold back the orgasm. on the way and very near now. Nothing in the world could stop it. It was a pity that it was coming so quickly but she would do better next time. It seemed that everything was going wrong today. First, she had not had the strentgth to deliver even fifty lashes. And now his orgasm had beaten her. Oh well, she thought, that had to happen sometimes. And he was so handsome and attractive. *That* was the reason, of course! *She* would win next time, never mind his handsomeness!

She played with his testicle bag with her long and shapely fingernails. She alternately scratched and punctured the skin. She waited breathlessly for the juices to enter her mouth.

At this precise moment they did so. They spurted to the back of her tongue, spurt after vigorous spurt.

Saunders felt his senses slipping away from him. He knew he was fainting from the ultimate of sensation. He was happy to do so. Any resisting action would have been something like blasphemy, so marvellous was the state in which he seemed to be floating.

Makasile half-closed her throat in order to trap the juices at the back of her mouth and let them be swalloowed slowly, lasciviously, languorously, wantonly... And as she swallowed them, her own juices mounted and exploded in her loins...

After what seemed an aeon of ecstasy, everything came to an end at last. She lifted her head, letting the penis slip out of her mouth. She sat quite still on her stool, waiting for her heart to resume its normal beat.

Salome had also reached her own fulfilment—in the nick of time. She had done something that was not strictly permitted, in order to help herself to have her orgasm. She had seen that Saunders was coming— and she had realised that she, though very near, was not quite ready. At the last moment she had stopped her frantic lashing and had knelt behind him. She had put her teeth to his bleeding buttocks and had bitten them hard, one after the other. And she had herself come almost at the same instant, with a ferocity that had shaken her. After it was over she had slipped to the floor. She lay there for some moments, trying to regain her breath. Then at last she stood up, went to the cabinet and poured more whisky.

Saunders was the first to speak. "I can do with that," he said, in a croaking tone, as Salome brought the two glasses towards the whipping post. He had the impression that he had either fainted and had an ecstatic dream, or that he had been momentarily translated into another form of life. At all events, he realised that something very special indeed had just happened to him. But he wanted the whisky very much indeed.

Salome handed a glass to Makasile. She waited obediently while it was drunk. Then she stood again on tip-toe and helped Saunders to drink his.

"Are you going to untie me now?" he asked. "I'm getting numb."

"Untie you?" echoed the girl. "What makes you think that I should?"

"Haven't you finished?"

She shook her head. "I shouldn't think so. You were sentenced to a major flogging, and you haven't had half of it yet." She laughed softly. "Don't count what I gave you myself. That was something extra." She glanced down at her mistress who was still sitting motionlessly on her stool. "I imagine Her Highness will want to deliver the rest of her flogging as soon as she has rested a little."

"But, for Christ's sake——" And then he stopped. What was the good of arguing? Whatever was going to happen would inevitably happen. He himself was powerless to stop it.

As though in answer to his thoughts, Makasile looked up slowly. There was an expression of exhausted peace on her face and in her eyes. "You must naturally have the rest of your flogging," she said. "But not today. I'm too tired."

So he was not going to be released! It was as he had thought.

"When must I have it?" he asked.

She appeared to concentrate. "Well, not tomorrow or the next day, because I shan't be here. Probably the day after that."

"But what am I supposed to do in the meantime?" he exploded. Now that he had had his orgasm he had forgotten that he had thought that it might be quite pleasant if he were not released at once.

Makasile smiled. "Salome," she said.

The girl bowed her head silently.

"Would you like to amuse yourself with him tomorrow and the next day?" asked Makasile.

"Oh, Highness," breathed the girl. "Yes please!"

"You may do so then."

"Look!" spluttered Saunders. "You're surely not serious—"

Makasile interrupted him. "The last time you used that expression was in relation to having your johnthomas flogged. And you know what happened then. I advise you to be quiet—or you may annoy me." She was beginning to feel a little irritable. She was very tired. She wanted to lie down and sleep for a long while.

Salome made a fluttering movement with her hands. "Highness?"

"Yes?"

"May I please use this room?"

Makasile thought for a moment. "I don't see why not. And if you want to bring any of the other girls, you can do that too."

"Oh, thank you, Highness." There was a look of fierce anticipation in her eyes already, as she made a rapid plan of what she would do the next day.

"Be careful, though," said Makasile. "Don't do too much to him. Don't kill him. I want him for myself for the day after tomorrow—and later."

He looked into her eyes. "And later," he echoed. "How much later?"

She looked back into his. "I can't tell you that," she said frankly.

"I mean, how long shall I have to stay here? When will you let me go?"

She gazed at him reflectively. "And I can't tell you that either. It needs a lot of thinking about. It's just possible that I may never be able to let you go. You know too much about me."

"Jesus Christ!" he whispered. He had been completely right.

"Wouldn't you like to stay," she said mischievously, "as my principal whipping boy?" Her expression suddenly changed. Her eyes became serious. "Tell me. Treat that as a serious question."

"Would I like to stay here," he repeated, "as your principal whipping boy?"

"Yes."

"And the whipping boy," he said acidly, "of all the servants in your palace."

"No, not necessarily."

"But you've just given permission to her to make a party of it tomorrow with her friends."

She laughed. "That could be rescinded. It depends on what I decide to do. The thing that worries me is that I don't see how I'm going to be able to let you go free. You might just talk to the newspapers, mightn't you? So it looks as though I must keep you here. But in what capacity? As a prisoner? Of course, that is possible. Everything is possible in Gubadan. Or as my principal whipping boy, with a certain amount of freedom? Or even"—she paused and looked at him meditatively—"as my lover?" She stood up abruptly. "We'll see what I feel like the day after tomorrow. In the meantime, Salome and the others can soften you up a bit more."

VI

SCREAM, MY DARLING, SCREAM!

A car was just driving away from the kerb as James Merridew turned into the road and looked for a place to park near the house to which he was invited.
"Very lucky," he murmured to himself, switching off his engine and lights. He got out of his car, locked it and ran across the pavement. As he went through the big gate, a crowd of people were coming down the steps of the house. He did not know them, but they nodded to him politely as he went past them. He returned their nods, reflecting with some amusement that a late arrival at a cocktail party sometimes amounts to a form of introduction.
"I'm sorry I'm so late," he told his hostess, as he entered the room in which she was saying goodnight to the early-departing guests.
"It's nice of you to come," she smiled. "Your wife told us that you had a last-minute office session. So you're off tomorrow?"
"Yes. Crack of dawn."
"How exciting. You must tell me all about it."

He moved aside as another wave of departing guests came up to her. "I'll see you later. Where's your husband?"

She waved her hand vaguely towards another room and shrugged her shoulders charmingly.

He found his wife inside the other doorway.

"Oh, hello, darling," she said. "So you made it."

He squeezed her hand. "Hello, sweet. Where's our host? Seen him?"

"In front of you—about five yards away."

He squinted into the crowd. "Oh yes. I'll go and say good evening."

"Come back to me then, will you?" she said. "I've been lonely."

He grinned at her, squeezed her hand again. "Be back in a jiffy."

When he had paid his respects to his host and was making his way back to his wife, he was waylaid by Mrs Bannister. He sighed inwardly.

Mrs Bannister was a woman who could be justly described as a battle-axe. But she had a certain heavy charm too. And she had the tendency of forming a strong liking for certain people. She had formed just such a strong liking for James Merridew and his wife at their wedding a month previously. "I have never seen," she had said on that occasion, "two young people more eminently suited to each other." She had paused and glared at her listeners. "You will notice that I said suited *to* each other, not *for* each other. And that makes a great difference." Her listeners had nodded theirs heads in wise and solemn agreement, wondering at the same time what, on earth she was talking about. Nobody had had the courage to ask her.

"I've just heard about it," Mrs Bannister now boomed in his ear.

"About what?" he smiled, although he knew what she meant.

She gave him a playful punch in the ribs. "This romantic honeymoon of yours. But I want all the details. Come on, tell me. Everything."

"That's a tall order," he said weakly. He looked around the room for his wife, caught her eye, nodded and smiled. "Let's go over and join Helena. And we'll both tell you in relays."

"You've only just arrived," she said, fixing him with an accusing glare.

"Yes," he admitted. "Last-minute clearing up. We're off tomorrow."

She gave a grunt. "Come on, then. Let's go to your poor wife. You're lucky to have a wife like that."

He silently agreed with her, but wondered what particular reason was at his moment in her mind.

"Mrs Bannister is interested in our trip," he said as they came up to Helena. "What shall we confess to her?" He realised that he was not sounding very clever, but cocktail parties always affected his conversational abilities.

"You're off tomorrow?" boomed Mrs Bannister. A few other guests turned to see who was off the next day, recognised Helena and James, grinned and returned to their own conversations.

"Yes," said Helena. "On the nine o'clock boat for Boulogne."

"And then?"

"We'll camp from then on, if it's possible. We may have to stay in a hotel in some of the towns, but it'll be our tent whenever possible."

Mrs Bannister fixed her with a stare. It had a good deal of affection in it, and Helena knew this, but it would have terrified anyone who did not know Mrs Bannister's mannerisms. "And you're really driving all the way to the Persian Gulf?"

"Yes."

"Why?"

"Why not?" James countered with a smile.

"Sounds rather grim. You'll be going through some outlandish parts."

"Oh, I don't think so. Everything is pretty civilised these days."

"What actually is your route?"

He looked at his wife. "Helena's turn now. She's the navigator."

Mrs Bannister frowned. "You mean to say you don't know the route?"

"Of course I know it," he said, slightly nettled. "But it's Helena's department."

"After France," said Helena, ticking off the countries on her fingers as she named them, "we go across Italy to Trieste, then down through Yugoslavia into Greece. At Salonika we head east again towards Turkey. Then we head across Turkey for Lebanon, Irak and—oh, a lot of desert. Then we arrive at the Persian Gulf."

"God willing," said Mrs Bannister ominously.

"Yes, God willing," replied Helena quietly.

Mrs Bannister suddenly regretted her remark. To make up for it she slapped James boisterously on the shoulder and boomed: "Love in the sun, eh? You devil, you!"

The people next to them turned again and smiled. A girl said: "Is this is your second honeymoon that she's teasing you about?"

The man next to her said: "What second honeymoon? Are the Merridews having another honeymoon?"

Helena laughed. "Not really a second one, you know. Our first one was only a long week end."

"And where are you spending it this time?" He had not taken in Mrs Bannister's boisterous joke.

"James has been posted to the Persian Gulf. So we're driving there in a Land Rover. We're going to take a month on the journey. Camping most of the time."

"Isn't that a bit dangerous?" asked the girl, drifting over to them and becoming part of their conversation. "Unfriendly tribes in the desert and so on."

James shook his head. "Not nowadays. Everything is pretty civilised and friendly."

"I have heard," said Mrs Bannister ponderously, "of a tribe called Moregs or Maregs or something—"

"Maregs," said James. "Yes, a tribe of desert nomads."

"And I have heard that it's very bad to be taken prisoner by them. Their women kill the prisoners very slowly with knives. They do the most awful things with their knives."

"I think," said James lightly, with a reassuring glance at his wife, "that sort of thing certainly *used* to happen. Last century. The sort of thing Wren wrote about so successfully." He offered his cigarette case around the group. "But I'm sure it doesn't happen nowadays."

"All the same," said the girl who had joined them, "I think you are awfully brave."

"So do I," agreed Mrs Bannister. "I wouldn't drive across those deserts for anything in the world." She glared at James. "What happens if your car breaks down."

"We radio for help," he said calmly.

"Oh, you carry radio?"

"Yes, a short-wave transmitter. So we're never really out of touch with the rest of the world." He smiled. "You see, it has become rather unromantically safe and secure." He said this to allay any doubts Helena might be having. She had already expressed certain fears of this journey, and he had argued them away. It was a nuisance that this Bannister woman was saying things like this.

Helena said suddenly, as though to tell him that she had not begun to worry again: "So it really *is* a case of love in the sun, as you said." She blushed slightly as the force of the double-entendre struck her.

Mrs Bannister chuckled. She liked double-entendres. She slapped James' shoulder again and growled: "Devil, you are! Oh well, I suppose you'll be safe enough. But I'll give you a letter to a friend of mine in Damascus. I suppose you're going through Damascus."

"Yes, we are," said Helena doubtfully. "And it's very kind of you—but we're off very early tomorrow morning."

"I doubt whether there'll be time for you to write it," said James, who felt that they really did not need any more letters of introduction, "or for us to pick it up."

"There'll be plenty of time to write it," said Mrs Bannister with resolution. "And you needn't pick it up. You'll be too busy with last-minute packing. Easy. I'll send it round to your flat tonight, before bed time."

"Extremely kind of you," murmured James. "Many thanks indeed."

"It will be useful to meet him," said Mrs Bannister. "He's a very powerful man in those parts. He might be able to help you—if you do land in trouble."

The letter arrived three hours later.

"Nice of the old horse, really," said James, glancing at the name and address on the envelope. "Good heavens! He has a tremendous title."

"Has he?" said Helena. "She did say that he's a powerful main in those parts. It might be useful to have him up our sleeve."

They were undressing for bed. He watched her slip off her petticoat and stand enticingly in her brassiere and panties. They were made of black silk and lace, and she looked very enticing indeed.

He went to her and put his hands under her armpits. He lifted her off the floor and, as her mouth came up to the level of his, kissed her.

She felt the hardness of his penis pressing against her like a large piece of wood. "There's another powerful man down there too," she murmured.

"Yes," he murmured back, now lightly biting her ear. "Let's do something about him, shall we?"

"I don't know where you get the energy," she said, with mock severity. She was in fact very proud of his virility. They had been married for little over a month, and he still made love to her three or four times a day.

"I'm a young 'un," he said, grinning. "That's where I get it from."

"You're thirty-one," she said teasingly, as though to suggest that he was no longer in his prime. "So I don't know where you get it!"

He roared with laughter. He swept her off her feet. He tossed her on the bed with seeming casualness but in fact with great care that she should fall well. "I'll now proceed to show you!" He stripped off the few clothes he was wearing. He threw himself over her.

"Where you get it from?" she said, seizing his penis and squeezing it hard. "Is that what you'll show me?"

"What?"

"You will now proceed to show me where you *get* it from?"

"No." He smoothed his hands over her breasts. "I'll now proceed to show you that I've *got* it!" He slipped his fingers under her brassiere. He felt for her firm, cool nipples. "That I've got it in abundance!"

She opened her legs and felt his penis slide nearer to its ultimate destination. "We shouldn't be doing this," she murmured. "We've got to get up early."

He moved his hips slightly in order to be able to push his penis into her without help from either his or her hand. He felt the knob coming into contact with her lips. He gave a little push with his thighs. He felt himself entering.

As always, she caught her breath sharply as she

felt the great thing enter her. She was a smallish girl—five feet five inches in height and very petite; and he was a very big man—six feet two inches, broad, muscular and with the penis—she sometimes thought—of a glorious bull.

It slid inside, bringing with it the heavenly sensations. She moaned.

She clutched at his shoulders. She sank her fingernails into his flesh. She said, dreamily: "You won't forget your promise?"

He said: "What promise?"

"About Marseilles."

He knew what she meant, but he said teasingly: "Marseilles? Marseilles? Now what could I have promised about Marseilles?"

She dug her nails more deeply into his shoulders. "Wretch! You'll take me, won't you?"

When they had been planning the itinerary of their journey a week or so before, she had asked him whether he had ever been to Marseilles before.

"Yes, once," he had answered. "During the war."

"Did you ever go," she had shyly asked, "to any of those rather wicked nightclubs?"

"You mean the places where they have shows?"

"Yes. Shows of people being whipped, and things like that."

He had paused. Then: "Yes," he said simply. "I went to one. Why do you ask?"

And she had surprised him. "I want to go to one too. Will you take me?"

"They're a bit shocking."

"Doesn't matter. I want to see this whipping business."

"Why?"

"Heard a lot about it."

"Good heavens! Where have you heard about it?"

"Oh, here and there," she said evasively. "The point is: will you take take me?"

"Certainly."

"You promise?"

"Yes, darling, I promise."

Now, she dug her nails deeply into his skin and repeated. "Come on! Or I'll tear you to bits. You promised, didn't you?"

He thrust his penis further into her vaginal passage.

"You *are* tearing me to bits already!"

"Promise again."

He laughed helplessly. "Yes, yes! I promise."

"As soon as we get to Marseilles?"

"Yes, the first night."

She released the pressure of her fingers. As she lifted them, it felt as though her nails had sunk themselves to their full length into his flesh—and they were very long nails. "All right," she said dreamily. "Just so long as we know where we are."

They set off the next morning at seven. They were in no hurry, and they saw no sense in driving long distances and, in consequence, getting on each other's nerves. James was not due in the Persian Gulf for more than a month.

They came to a stop each evening at about seven o'clock—either at a camping ground near some small town or by the side of a stream in the open country. It was now three-quarters of the way through September and the summer crowds had all gone home. They found themselves almost alone even in the camping grounds. This suited them well, for they made love very often—and they wanted as much privacy as they could get.

They would put up their tent—a largish one designed for five or six people—and open a bottle of wine. After that, James would busy himself with the connection of the tent light to the battery of the Land Rover, with the setting up of the table and chairs, and with the various other sundry jobs connected with the erection of a camp. While he was doing this, Helena pumped up the rubber air mattresses. She did not pump them up very hard, for, she said: "There's something heavenly about making love on a ruber air mattress. It's like making love on a cloud. But it must be very soft if it *is* going to be like a cloud."

They had some more wine and retired inside the tent. They closed the flaps carefully, in case any inquisitive child might pass by. They stripped each other—slowly and lasciviously removing one garment after another—and feeling a tremendous appetite of sex building up inside them. They lay on the soft cloud-like air mattresses. They entwined their arms and legs around each other, and copulated deliciously.

After some minutes of relaxation, they got up, put on some clothes, and opened up the tent flaps. Helena then cooked something for supper. Afterwards, they sat relaxed, at peace, and very much in love.

And after an hour of so of sitting in the romantic light of the tent lamp, James, feeling randy again, took Helena by the arm and led her into the tent. She, feeling equally randy, lay quickly down on the air mattresses and held out her arms to him.

They reached Marseilles on the evening of their fourth day out from England. They felt that they had dawdled a little too much on the first leg of their journey. If it had not been for his promise to take Helena to a certain type of night club, James would have suggested that they should drive on at least as far as Toulon. But they had taken the long way round, specifically in order to take in Marseilles...

They did not attempt to find any camping ground. In a big city, it was not so pleasant to put up their tent. They went at once to a hotel that James had once stayed at.

"I think I'd better go and make a recce," he said, when they were finished with their love-making.

"Recce? What's that?"

"Reconnaissance. A military expression," he said, a little pompously. "I mean I'd better go and find out whether that night club still exists."

"Yes," she said, looking at him thoughtfully. "I suppose you'd better. I hope it does. What are we going to do if it's been closed up? After looking forward to it so much, too!"

He grinned. "You're really awful, you know."

"Darling, yes," she admitted. "I know I am. But I do want to see people whipping each other."

He stared at her curiously. "*Why* do you?"

She shook her head. "I don't know."

"Have you any personal interest in it, perhaps?"

"Personal? No, I don't think so."

He grinned again. "I mean, you wouldn't like me to give you one?"

"A whipping? No, of course not," she said forcefully. She did not, however feel as forceful as she made herself sound. In some ways, it was quite an exciting thought to be given a whipping by James. But she couldn't possibly tell him that.

"Or is it that *you* would like to give *me* one?" he asked.

Now *that*, she suddenly decided, was also an exciting idea—but equally impossible to confess. "Of course not, darling," she said, stroking his hair. "It's just that I've heard of these places—and I'd like to complete my education. That's all, I assure you." And she felt annoyed with herself for apologising. "After all," she went on, somewhat aggressively, "you've completed your own education with them, haven't you?"

"Yes, yes, darling girl," he said soothingly, seeing that she was becoming nervy.

She forced a smile. "So what's sauce for the goose is—"

"Yes, sweetheart. Sauce for the gander. But you've got your sexes mixed up a bit. You're the goose—I'm the gander."

Her irritation fell away completely. "All right, my gander. Go and do your recce. Don't be too long, though."

James took a taxi outside the hotel. He did not remember the name of the street in which the night club had been situated, but he remembered the general direction and directed the taxi driver as he went along.

In the place where it had been there was now a block of flats.

He stared at the place and felt sorry that Helena was going to be so disappointed.

A waterfront loafer sidled up to him. "Looking for the night club that was here?" he asked in French.

James glanced at him. Normally he would have been too shy to admit it, but the thought of Helena's disappointment gave him courage. "Yes," he said, squinting up at the building again. "Seems to have gone."

"It's still working."

"Good. Do you know where?"

"Yes."

"Will you tell me?"

"Depends."

James pulled out his wallet. He extracted some notes.

The loafer glanced at them. "It still depends."

"How much do you want?"

The man named a figure that was foolishly exorbitant.

"Go to hell," said James, and put his wallet back into his pocket. It was a great pity that Helena would be disappointed—and so would he, he now reflected—but such a price was out of the question. He walked away abruptly

As he crossed the street, a thought came to him. At the corner there was a small general store—the type of shop that sold everything: food and vegetables and pans and brushes and buckets. He remembered that they needed a good many things for their tent, as well as a lot of new provisions for the next part of their journey.

As he had hoped. the shop keeper was a man. James gave his orders, one after the other. The goods were piled up on the counter. He asked how much the total was. It was rather less than the sum that the loafer had demanded.

James brought out his wallet. "Can you tell me, please," he asked, pleasantly, "where the night club is now—that one that used to be opposite?"

The shopkeeper's face became expressionless. "What night club, m'sieur?"

James sighed. "It's a pity—and I'm ashamed to—to"—he struggled to remember the French word for 'blackmail' but failed—"to behave like this, but I *must* have that information." He put his wallet back into his pocket, his eyes on the pile of goods on the counter.

The shop keeper shrugged. "Eh bien! In the same circumstances I might do the same thing." He gave James an address.

James thanked him warmly, paid for his goods, on an impulse bought a few more things, and left the shop heavily laden.

Helena was not going to be disappointed.

Nor was he.

The amount of money that he had to pay at the doorway staggered James for a moment. He bore up manfully, however, paid it, and led Helena downstairs to a large underground room.

At the foot of the stairs they were met by a pretty girl who escorted them to a table in a curtained alcove.

Helena opened her eyes wide at the way this girl was dressed.

She wore a very short skirt that was made of a large number of leather shoe-laces, and she had no panties on beneath this frill-like covering. Her breasts were almost naked, only the nipples being covered by a round piece of soft kid. Around her wrists and ankles were two-inch-wide buckles of similar soft kid. On her feet were shoes with very high stiletto heels.

In her right hand she carried a menu. In her left there was a whip.

Helena blinked at the sight of this whip. She knew that the place was a special one for exhibitions of various forms of flagellation, but, somehow, she was unprepared for the sight of a waitress carrying a whip. Her heart gave a tremulous bound. She gripped James's hand.

They sat down in their alcove and looked around the room.

The nearly naked waitress called their attention by doubling her whip in her left hand, putting it prominently on to the table, and saying politely: "Would m'sieur like to order?" She gave James the menu with her right hand.

As he had suspected, he found that all the drinks were prohibitively expensive, but after only a moment's hesitation he ordered a magnum of champagne. They might as well enjoy themselves, he thought.

Tables similar to theirs, curtained and private, ran round the dance-floor. This was about five yards square. In its centre there was a stout post about six feet tall. The post was of about the thickness of a man's leg.

"We shouldn't need three guesses," said Helena, with a shiver of pure, delicious excitement, "to know what that is for, should we?"

James had been staring at it. In the previous night-club there had been nothing like it, but, as Helena had said, it was not difficult to guess what it was to be used for. He began to feel extremely excited.

Their champagne arrived. The waitress slipped the loop of the whip over her left wrist, in order to open the bottle of champagne. She looked at James intently all the time she was doing so. Her eyes were burning.

Helena noticed this but—to her own surprise—did not feel resentful. In such a place as this, conventions had to be thrown overboard. So, if this waitress seemed to hunger for her husband—well, it was all part of the atmosphere. She picked up her glass and drained it.

The waitress re-filled it at once.

"Madame will enjoy herself?" she said—but it was more of a statement than a question. From politeness to a foreigner, she enunciated her words carefully, in case the foreigner should not understand her.

It was not necessary. Helena had been at a French finishing school and her French was even better than James's. "I hope so," she murmured. "When does everything begin?"

"In three or four minutes, madame." Her eyes flickered back to James and seemed to drink him in.

Helena ignored this. "Are you part of the show?" she asked pleasantly.

The girl nodded. "Yes, madame." She did not take her eyes away from James however. Then she said: "Would you also like to be part of the show, m'sieur?"

James was not listening to her. He realised that she and Helena were having some sort of conversation, but he was taking no notice. He was looking at the post in the centre of the floor, and wondering whether a man or a girl would be tied to it. He understood that the girl had said something to him. "I beg your pardon," he said swiftly, looking up at her with a smile.

The girl looked down at him smoulderingly. Her

149

nostrils dilated slightly. James saw this and realised that he had made a conquest. Helena was taking another swig of champagne. Nevertheless she too noticed the smouldering look.

"I asked m'sieur," said the girl, fixing him straight in the eyes with a challenging gaze, "whether he would like to be part of the show."

"In what way?" James gazed back at her curiously. "To do what?"

She motioned with her whip. "I am going to use this."

"So?"

"I should be happy if m'sieur would volunteer to have me use it on him."

James's gaze changed into a stare of astonishment. "Use that on me?" He pointed his finger at the whip. "That thing?"

The girl smiled. "Yes, m'sieur."

"You're crazy," said James shortly.

Helena giggled. She had drunk a little too much before they arrived at this night club, and the champagne was now beginning to affect her. "I don't mind, darling. If you want to, go ahead."

He frowned. "Don't be silly." He lit a cigarette nervously.

At this moment, a band—whose existence they had not yet suspected—began to play a piece with a violent, savage tempo. There was a pause of a moment and then a door at the end of the room began to open slowly. The lights dimmed. A spotlight played on the door. The tempo rose to a crescendo.

The waitress moved quickly to the door of the alcove. "I must go. I'm in the show. But I'll be back, m'sieur. I want to use my whip on you."

Helena reached for his hands. "You've made such a hit!"

He grinned a little shyly. "It seems so."

"But, darling, you should have accepted her."

He frowned again. "Are you a little bitsy tight, my sweet?"

"Yes," she said. "But not very. And she's fallen head over heels for you. I wouldn't have minded."

"She wanted to use that whip on me."

"Of course. That's what I meant."

He glared at her, and then suddenly softened. He filled both their glasses to the brim. "You're getting as tight as a tick, but I know why."

"Why?"

"You're feeling a bit embarrassed by all this."

Helena put her glass to her lips, and nodded her head. "You know me too well, darling."

"Don't be."

She drank a gulp. "No, of course not."

"But don't get too tight."

"No."

"Otherwise you'll not enjoy anything."

Helena gave herself a shake. "You're quite right." She stared at the door on which the spotlight still played, the music rising and falling in a continuing aggravation of suspense. "Why don't they start something?"

At that moment they did.

The door opened wide. Four girls danced on to the floor. Among them was their waitress. They all wore short skirts made of thin strips of leather. None of them wore panties: that was very clearly seen at once. They all had round pieces of kid over their nipples. They all wore shoes with dangerously high stiletto heels. They were all very pretty. And they all carried whips.

They danced round the floor two or three times, making slashes with their whips to the tempo of the music.

James began to feel randy. He was surprised at this, for he had no masochism in him—as far as he knew. But nevertheless the sight of the four very pretty whip-bearing girls on the floor excited him.

Helena sat watching with wide open eyes. She too was feeling very randy. And she too was surprised at herself. All sorts of previously buried thoughts, emotions and desires began to take hold of her. She found herself wishing that she was one of the girls on the floor.

The music came to another crescendo, and stopped. The girls stood still.

One of them stepped towards the post. She put her hand on it and smiled provocatively at the alcoves all round the floor. The occupants of the alcoves could all be seen by her. They could not be seen by one another.

"And now, messieurs," she said. "Who will be the first volunteer?"

There was a sort of groan of pent-up passion around the room, but nobody volunteered.

Helena opened her mouth to tell James to go ahead and volunteer, but changed her mind. Something suddenly sobered her up. She realised at last precisely what was going to happen. She shivered deliciously, felt for James's hand across the table, and settled down to watch with great interest.

"But, messieurs!" said the girl at the post. "Where is your manliness?"

"Let a girl volunteer," shouted some man from an alcove a few yards away. "I'd rather see a girl being whipped."

The girl at the post turned at once to him. "Ah, monsieur, you would like to see a girl being whipped? Then may I ask your companion if she will volunteer?" She left the post and walked to the alcove from which the man had spoken. She said, smilingly: "Madame? Will madame volunteer to be whipped?"

Evidently she received a negative answer, for she turned on her heel impatiently and addressed the whole room again. "Is there not *one* real man present, messieurs?"

"Yes!" shouted a voice on the other side of the room. "I will volunteer! I can take anything that the four of you can give."

There was an audible murmur of relief around the whole room. It was as though everybody present had been in an agony of suspense lest he himself should become the victim he had come to watch.

The four girls approached the alcove from which the voice had come. They held out their hands to help the volunteer to climb over the rail that separated his alcove from the floor.

He was a man of about thirty years of age, well-built, moderately tall, and very good looking. He walked without any self-consciousness to the middle of the floor.

"I suppose you want me to take my clothes off," he said.

"We'll do that," said the girl who seemed to be the leader. "Just stand there and relax."

The other three girls came up to him. They slipped the loops of their whips over their wrists. They began to undress him, garment by garment.

In a very short space of time he was standing naked in the middle of the floor, three or four feet away from the post. His penis was greatly erected.

The leader walked to where the band was sitting, half-hidden. She cupped her hands. A length of stout rope and a length of thin silk cord were thrown to her. She came back to the volunteer victim. She took his penis in her hand and pulled him by it towards the post.

"Open your legs," she said distinctly, so that all the audience should hear. "I'm going to tie this silk cord round you ball bag."

"Why?"

"In order to immobilise you completely."

"I don't understand you."

The girl laughed. "You will, m'sieur, you will! Just open your legs."

The volunteer did as she told him. "But—" he began.

"You will understand in a moment." She made a loop in the silk cord and passed the loop over his testicles. She drew the loop tight at the base of the testicle bag. "Now are you beginning to see?" She looked up at him with flashing eyes.

He seemed genuinely puzzled, although a fair number of the audience must already have guessed what was going to happen to him.

Helena thought she knew, but she felt too shy to admit it even to James. "What is she doing?" she asked innocently.

"I think," said James, his own penis mightily erected, "that she is going to tie him up by his balls to that post."

"My God!" breathed Helena. This was exactly what she had thought. "Isn't it terribly dangerous?"

"It will be if he moves."

"But they're going to whip him, aren't they?"

"I suppose so."

"And if they whip him so hard that he jumps, he'll injure himself."

James gave a short laugh. "He won't only injure himself if he does any moving—he'll kill himself. But he asked for it, you know."

"I wonder if he realised how they were going to tie him up."

"Probably not. But he's learning now."

The girl who had tied the silk cord round the base of his testicle bag pulled on the loop to tighten it as much as possible. She beckoned him to stand as near as possible to the post. She made a final attempt to make the loop even tighter, and then passed the free ends round the posts. She pulled these very tight, and tied them. His penis was drawn very close against the post. She gave it a swift caress and said, loud enough for everybody to hear. "And now you have seen, haven't you?"

Helena said suddenly: "He may be part of the act."

James nodded. "He may, at that. But it seems he's going to have a good deal of pain. Those whips don't look at all soft and gentle."

"They don't," said Helena, gazinz at them hungrily. She wished she possessed one. She could not have said why, or what use she would have put it to. She only knew that she wished she could have one of her own.

She suddenly shook her head, as though to clear it of such thoughts. She had certainly had too much to drink. She must be careful. She must keep a watch on her words and her actions, or else she might shock James dreadfully.

The girl at the post was holding out the length of rope. "Put your hands round the post," she ordered the volunteer victim.

"Am I not sufficiently helpless already?" He pulled very gently with his hips, and stopped pulling at once. Like that he would castrate himself.

"Oh yes," she said. "But your back and legs and bottom are going to be the main places whipped. If you put your hands behind you to try to protect yourself it would be a waste of time, of course. But it would also be a bit of a nuisance for us, too. So we'd rather have your hands safely tied up out of the way. So do as I say. Put your hands round the post. I want to tie them."

"I see," he said shortly, and watched her tying his wrists together on the far side of the post. He began to wonder whether he had been wise to volunteer.

"How much of a masochist are you?" she asked, in a loud clear voice.

"A masochist? I don't know what you mean." He pulled ineffectually on his hands.

She sighed. "You volunteered, didn't you?"

"Yes, I volunteered."

"Why did you?"

He looked at her blankly.

She said patiently. "You volunteered because you like—or liked—the idea of being whipped by us girls. Isn't that it?"

"Yes," he said at once. "That's it." *And,* he told himself, it will be fun.

"That means you're a masochist." She blew out her cheeks a little impatiently. "Look up the word in your dictionary when you get home. It means someone who likes to receive physical pain. The point is: *how much* of a masochist are you?"

"Why? Why do you have to know?" This girl talked a lot too much.

"I must know," she said, her tone one of exaggerated patience, "because if you're not a very advanced masochist we must gag you. We don't want your screams to reach the street and bring the police."

"I shan't scream," he said, with an air of injured pride. "I can take anything you can dish out." I bloody well can, he told himself aggressively.

"All of us?" She glanced at the three other girls who were smiling cruelly.

"All of you—and I'll whistle a song too, at the same time."

Helena drank a sip of champagne. "You know, darling, I don't believe he can possibly be part of the act."

"I agree with you," said James.

"He's so brash. So cocky—and unpleasant. If he were part of the act, he would surely have been given better lines to say."

"That's more or less what I thought."

"And yet I feel rather sorry for him."

"Why?"

"I don't really know. Probably because he's bitten

off more than he can chew. Of course, he must be a bit perverted." She stopped, wondering after all whether it was *really* so perverted to want to whip and be whipped.

"Of course he's perverted!" said James forcefully.

"Is that a reason to feel sorry for him?"

"No, of course not, but—"

"But what, darling?"

"He's probably had too much to drink—as I have—and he volunteered in that mad way—and he didn't realise what was going to happen to him—and—and—oh, I don't know!"

James felt for her hand. "Sweetheart, you are letting your famous sympathy for dumb animals get the better of you."

She smiled at him quizzically. "Am I?"

"You are. You are, indeed. And I can prove it."

"Go ahead and prove it. I'll be very happy to stop feeling sorry for him. But I doubt whether you can prove it. I think he is just someone who has drunk too much, and has got himself into an awful situation—and wants to get out of it, and can't."

"Look at his penis."

"What?"

"His penis, darling. You can just see it, can't you?"

She craned her head sideways. "Yes, I can see it."

"Is it erected or not?"

She chuckled. "All right, you win. With such an erection as that, he is in no need of sympathy from anyone. Okay, you win. And things are beginning to happen."

He filled their glasses, congratulating himself for ordering a magnum rather than a bottle. A bottle would have been empty by now, and their waitress was very busy...

The band struck up again. It did not play any melody. It played rhythm. And the rhythm made the pulses of the audience beat with lustful anticipation.

The girls with the whips began a frightening sort of dance round the man who was helpless at the post, tied tightly by his testicles to the wood and unable to make the slightest movement.

He eyed them fearfully as they danced round him, swishing their whips through the air, ever nearer and nearer to his naked body. Again he wondered whether he had been wise to put himself into this position. He began to think not.

The tempo of the music increased in speed. The swishes of the whips came nearer to him. Any moment now they would be laid across his flesh.

"Oh God!" breathed Helena. "Poor man. But why don't they *start,* if they're going to?"

James let out a great breath. "I agree. The tension is awful." He was feeling very surprised at himself. He had never before considered his own feelings in relation to flagellation. He knew it went on, but it didn't interest him personally. And that had been all. Now, looking at the fascinating scene on the floor: the four nearly-naked and very pretty girls, the swishing of their whips, the intoxicating beat of the rhythm, and the naked helpless man at the post—now he realised that it did after all interest him personally. His heart was beating fast. He wanted the whipping to begin. He wanted to see the whips cutting into that helpless back and bottom.

And there was something else that surprised him very much. He had had a queer thought deep down in his subconscious ever since the waitress had asked him to be part of the show, to let her use her whip on him. He had reacted conventionally, angrily. He had even been angry with Helena for her light-hearted and half-tipsy permission. But he had felt a sudden prickle of excitement too. He had forced it away. It was too ridiculous. He must have drunk too much, too, he told himself.

When he had watched the volunteer victim being

stripped by the girls, the prickle of excitement returned. And when the silk cord was tied round the victim's testicle bag the queer thought came to him that he might himself be in that position now, if he had accepted the waitress's proposition, and it might not be so terrible as it looked... It might be rather exciting to be whipped by those girls... He thrust the thought away angrily—cursing himself for drinking too much, and yet knowing very well that he had not yet drunk too much.

Now, with his usual characteristic of open-minded self-analysis, he stopped thrusting the thought away. He let it march forward, as it were—to occupy his brain like an invading army.

He was definitely identifying himself with the naked helpless victim at the post. He wished he were himself tied there by his testicles, waiting to be whipped by the girls.

There it was. That was the thought! It was out in all its colours!

He examined it carefully.

Yes, it *would* be rather exciting to be there, in the place of the victim! It was a pity that he hadn't accepted the waitress's offer.

But it was something he had better keep to himself. It would never do for Helena to know it.

On the other hand, *why* should he feel this? Was he a masochist after all? Had he always been a masochist—and had never realised it?

It seemed so.

Well, well, well, he thought to himself. This is not so good, is it?

"Why are you frowning?" asked Helena suddenly.

He smiled at once. "Am I? I suppose I want them to get on with the thing. This leading up to it and never quite getting there is very bad for the nerves." He was sorry that he could not tell her the truth.

Helena laughed. "Yes, it is. But I think they're just about getting there now."

She was right. The four girls were dancing much nearer now to the victim. Their whips swished through the air very near to his body, almost—but not quite—touching it.

Suddenly the whips struck his flesh.

Following each swishing sound there was now a crack as the lash cut into his back and bottom and legs.

Helena drew a long trembling breath. She had herself been surprised at some of the thoughts which were passing through her own mind.

During the preliminaries of the stripping and the tying up of the victim she had begun to ask herself whether it was after all *such* a perverted thing to want to whip—like their waitress; or to want to be whipped—like the man now tied to the post on the floor. She felt in her bones that it was wrong, bad, perverted. But she also felt that this was her prudery speaking, her careful, conventional upbringing... her Englishness. She knew from hearsay that the more hot-blooded of her fellow creatures often indulged in a sex whipping as a matter of course. To them, at any rate, there was nothing wrong with it, nothing perverted.

She thought, with a quiver of excitement, that she would like to be one of the girls on the floor. She would like to be lashing that male body at the post.

She suddenly sucked in her breath. A startling thought had struck her.

Suppose she were indeed one of the girls—*and suppose the victim were James!*

She put a hand over her heart. It was thumping furiously.

James to be tied up at the post!

And she herself to be dancing round him, wearing the same sort of short skirt of thin strips of leather, the same buckles round her wrists and ankles, the same high-heeled shoes—and with the same sort of whip in her hand...

Oh God!

She glanced at him. What *would* he say! Whatever would he think? She could imagine his shock of sheer outrage if she told him what she wanted to do. *"What she wanted to do?"* Had it become so clear in her mind already? Was that really what she was thinking?

Yes, she admitted to herself, it was exactly that that she had been thinking.

So, what was she going to do?

She gazed at the orgiastic scene in front of her, the thoughts having raced through her head so fast that the whipping was still only at its very beginning. Not more than half a dozen lashes had actually struck the body of the victim.

What, she repeated to herself, was she going to do? It was obvious that she had certain curious desires buried inside her—had had them, no doubt, all her life. And now they were thrusting themselves up to her consciousness. Should she thrust them away? There lay danger. That was the way people became frustrated and unhappy. Should she then let them come—and fill her mind— and influence her future sexual life?

If she did that, what would James say, and think? For, if she let these desires possess her, she would have to buy a whip and somehow persuade him to allow her to use it on him... to allow her to beat him, thrash him...

She shook her head. Oh no, that would never do! He would probably leave her, much as he loved her. No, the thing had to be buried. The desires had to be stifled at once, before they grew too strong. It would be best, in fact, to leave the place at once. But that would be such a pity... She had seen how expensive had been their entrance tickets. Perhaps they should stay and see what there was to be seen—and then forget all about it.

The victim at the post began to make moaning noises as the whips cut into his flesh, and as his blood began to run from the weals.

Helena felt her heart begin to pound even faster than it had been doing. The sound of the moans made her head swim with delirious excitement. She found herself wishing that he would begin screaming...

As she realised that she was indeed wishing such a thing, she flushed momentarily with shame. She shook her head again. They would simply have to go. This whole thing was becoming too much to bear. In another moment she would want to be put on the floor of the alcove and poked.

A fair number of the other guests in the adjacent and facing alcoves had in fact already begun to amuse themselves physically in various ways as they watched the orgy on the floor.

In the alcove exactly opposite them, she could see that the man had slipped his trousers down to his knees, had taken his partner on to his lap, and was sitting with his penis obviously buried inside her.

"Why do you keep shaking your head like that?" asked James.

She blushed in the half-darkness. She was glad that he would not be able to see the blush. "Was I shaking my head?" she asked, in as innocent a tone of voice as possible.

He was not deceived. "You were—and you know it! Come on. Tell me. What were you thinking?"

She gestured towards the alcove opposite them. This would have to serve as an explanation. She couldn't possibly tell him the truth. "Do you see what they're doing?"

He stared across the half-darkened room. "Good God, yes!"

"Now you understand." She was sorry to be untruthful, but there was nothing for it.

He chuckled. "That's a very good idea. Come here, wench! It is nothing to shake your head at. We'll do it ourselves." He unzipped his fly, pulled out his penis and testicles, and held out his hand for her.

"This is dreadfully wicked," she murmured happily, lifting up her skirt and pushing her panties down to her knees. "It's really bad."

"It is, isn't it?" he said, pulling her on to his lap, opening his legs a little, manipulating hers, nosing his penis towards her vagina, thrusting it in, and sitting back in his chair, his genital organ warmly and wetly encompassed by her soft, exciting passage.

She bit his ear lightly.

"Ow!" he exclaimed.

"Cissy!" she said. "That didn't hurt."

"It hurt very much."

"Nonsense. What do you think *he* is feeling now?" And she gestured towards the man who was tied to the post, and who was groaning and moaning more piteously now. "He is being hurt. Really hurt." And I wish I could hurt you like that, she thought. I wish I could thrash you, flog you, whip you, beat you, torture you, flay you, lash you, scourge you—her mind ran swiftly through all the exciting verbs—knout you, and—oh, whip you, whip you, whip you!" She put her teeth to his ear again and bit it much harder.

"OW!" he exclaimed very loudly. "Don't do that!"

"Sorry, darling," she said contritely. "I'm getting very excited."

"With this whipping business?" It would be interesting to know what she felt about the whole thing now. She had wanted to come to see it, but the actuality might be a bit more than she had bargained for: a bit too shocking.

"Yes," she said slowly, and cautiously. "With the whipping business—and everything else. The whole atmosphere is rather exciting, isn't it?"

"You're not sorry we came?"

Now that, she thought to herself, is a difficult question to answer, isn't it? If their coming to this place tonight resulted in a terrible frustration of always wanting to flagellate her husband, and never being able to do so—then she was very sorry they had come. But if their coming resulted in an additional and extremely exciting activity being added to their sexual life—she was very glad they had come. "Yes and no," she said, with a good deal of honesty.

He did not, of course, realise that she was being very honest. He misunderstood her. "Shall we go then, darling girl? Do you want to go?"

She put her arms round his neck and hugged him. "Whenever you want to—but not perhaps immediately. Let's see whether he will begin to scream."

He sighed as he saw how difficult it was to understand even his own wife. "Do you *want* him to begin screaming?" he asked curiously. There had been something in her voice which was intriguing.

She was saved from the necessity of a reply. At this moment the victim stopped moaning and began to shriek. Peal after shrieking peal tore through the room.

At once the band increased the tempo of the music.

The girls increased the speed of their dance and their lashes.

The shrieks increased in intensity.

Swish——laskk! Swish——crakkk! Swish——lashhhkk!

Scream after scream after scream...

Electrified by the new speed of events, James felt his orgasm coming quickly—running—racing—galloping...

Helena's own orgasm matched his in rhythm, beat and speed...

Swish——laskk! Scream!
Swish——crakkk! Scream after scream after scream... It was as though the screaming had deprived everyone in the place of his power of thought, of reasoning—of his sense of safety and danger.

No one thought that these terrible screams might reach the street. Everybody was too much interested in his or her own fulfilment of the delight that the screams were bringing.

The girls continued to dance in a near delirium—and to thrash in a frenzy of rapture.

The customers in the alcoves made violent love—some sitting on the other's lap, some on the floor, some over the tables...

Even the manager, who had been taking money at the door upstairs, was now standing beside the floor, his hands masturbating his penis as he watched the terrible whipping and listened to the ear-splitting screams.

Nobody thought of the danger of the police.

And then suddenly the police arrived.

There was a shrill whistling sound at the head of the stairs and a commotion as a number of heavy feet clattered down to the room where everything was happening.

At this moment, Helena and James were entering the culmination of their orgasms. As from far off they heard the whistles and the commotion, but they paid no attention. They clung to each other in rapturous bliss as their genitals pulsated simultaneously with their fulfilment. They did not even notice that the screaming had stopped.

Suddenly all the lights went out.

James realised at last that something was happening—something to which he should pay attention, but he was still in too much of that dreamy, blissful condition that follows an orgasm to be able to concentrate.

Then there was a voice, and a thin pencil of light from a torch. "Come on! Follow me!" It was the voice of their waitress. "Quickly! We're being raided. Follow me at once. I may be able to get you out at the back of the place."

Helena came to life like an electric wire as she realised what the girl was saying. She jumped off Jame's lap, pulled up her panties, grabbed his hand and said, breathlessly: "Come on, Jamie. Never mind your fly."

He ran after her out of the alcove, along the corridor and in the direction opposite the one from which they had entered. The waitress ran swiftly ahead of them, her torch held behind her to show them the way. She came to a door, unlocked it, opened it, held it for them to pass through. They ran past her into a narrow area with rubbish bins. A flight of stone steps led up to the street. They turned, hesitatingly, waiting for her to come.

"Go! Get away quickly!" she said, from the doorway.

"Aren't you coming too?" asked Helena.

"Yes, why not?" said James.

The girl shook her head. "No, of course not. I belong to the team. I must go back to them."

"But won't there be awful trouble for you?" James was only just beginning to realise how much she had done for them, in bringing them to this back way out. "Hadn't you better come with us?" He saw in the half light that she was still holding her whip.

She shook her head. "There won't be any trouble. Just a little fine, that's all. We're not really doing anything very badly wrong."

He said: "Well, thank you very much for getting us out. I wish"—he put his hand into his pocket to take out his wallet—"I wish I could—"

She smiled. "No, thank you, m'sieur. It was a pleasure. But you must go quickly. Don't stand here talking."

"You're right," said James. "I wish I could reward you in some way, that's all." He was walking up the steps behind Helena.

"There's a way, m'sieur," said the girl softly. "If you *want* to reward me."

He stopped and looked down at her. "What's the way? I like to, if possible."

"Oh, it's possible and easy. Just come back here another night, m'sieur—and let me use my whip on you." He heard her suck in her breath sharply. "You're my type, m'sieur. It's a pity you're married—but your wife might let me whip you one day."

The woke up late the next morning. When they woke, not knowing that the other was yet awake, they lay still—each thinking deep and difficult thoughts.

James was thinking of the last words of the girl. So he was her type, was he? And the thing she wanted to do to him was to give him a whipping—probably tied up by his balls as the other man had been.

The thought was undeniably exciting. But it was also unfaithful to his beloved Helena. It must therefore be put away and buried for ever.

It was a very great pity, though, that Helena did not have the same desires as the girl with the whip.

Helena lay on her back in her bed and remembered the last words of the girl, too. She burned with irritation that the girl could so easily express her wish, while she, the wife—with all the right in the world to express it, could not find the words.

Oh, it was very irritating indeed! And very frustrating.

Why couldn't she just say casually to James: "By the way, Jamie dear, it's not only that girl who'd like to whip you. I'd like to do so myself." Why was it so impossible to say that?

He would have a fit. That was the trouble.

But *would* he? He had seemed just as interested as

she in all that flagellation at the night club. It was just possible, wasn't it, that he had been having the same reactions as she?

Oh dear, she thought. It was all very complicated. But a way must be found. That was certain. Somehow or other she must lead him into accepting a whipping from her.

But things must be taken in the right order. First, she must buy some sort of suitable whip.

Later in the morning, she found a smart leather store in the centre of the city. She went in, wondering whether it sold whips of the sort she wanted.

James had told her at breakfast that he had various odd checks to make on the Land Rover, and would have to leave her alone for an hour or so. She had at once said that she had some shopping to do.

Neither of them had spoken of the events of the evening before. It was as though the one was waiting for the other to open the subject—and neither was willing to open it. But as the time went by and it was not discussed, it became obvious that something unusual was in the air. Something would very soon have to be said—in order to clear the air.

"Madame?" A shop assistant bowed to her as she entered the store.

"Do you sell whips?" she asked in her excellent French.

He looked a little startled. "Whips, madame?"

She saw his startlement, and at once felt embarrassed. "Riding whips, switches, and so on."

He looked relieved. "Yes, madame. On the first floor. Perhaps you will take the lift."

"The first floor? Oh no, I'll walk. Thank you."

She walked up the stairs, feeling angry with herself for being embarrassed. For heavens' sake, if one wanted a whip—and a *real* whip, not a riding whip or a switch—

why shouldn't one ask for it without being embarrassed? It was none of their business what one wanted it for.

An assistant approached her as she entered the first-floor showroom. "May I help you, madame?" He looked her up and down appreciatively. A most desirable customer. Desirable and exceptionally bed-worthy. He would try to draw out the proceedings with her as long as possible. It had been a boring morning so far. This lovely creature would perhaps compensate for it.

Helena noticed his lascivious look. She felt very angry. Really, this was not her morning! First, she had behaved like an idiot downstairs, getting herself into a state of totally unnecessary embarrassment. Now, here was this idiotic-looking salesman preening himself all over her and obviously undressing her with his eyes. She began to shake with anger. It was simply too much.

"Yes," she said coldly. "You can help me. I want to buy a whip."

"Madame?" He looked as startled as the man downstairs.

"Yes?" She was damned if she would explain again. "Didn't you understand?"

"Did madame say she wanted a whip?"

Helena fixed him with an angry stare. "Madame did. Are you capable of serving her, or shall she ask to be served by someone else?"

The salesman swallowed. The glorious creature seemed to be in a very bad temper. But it only made her even more attractive. He looked at her with seeming deference, but at the same time drinking in her tumultuous loveliness. "I hope I am capable of serving madame. May I ask what sort of a whip madame desires? For riding perhaps? Or"—he tittered suggestively—"for something else?"

"Yes," said Helena succinctly, and much to her own surprise. "For beating a man with. I suppose you sell those too."

The salesman blinked at her. Then his eyes opened wide. He tried to smile, failed, blushed, and turned away to hide his confusion. It was the first time in all his experience as a lecher that he had been outmanœuvred and routed. He was glad that none of his fellow salesmen were within earshot.

"What is the matter?" she asked, in a clear voice. "Do your or don't you sell that kind of whip?" She saw that two or three other customers were looking curiously at her, but she was beginning to be carried away by her own bravado. And it was easy, she suddenly realised. Just take a deep breath and say what you want to say. With enough breath behind it, it comes out easily enough! She thought of James and determined to apply the system when she got back to the hotel. She would take a deep breath—and show him the whip. Then she would take another breath and tell him what she wanted to do with it. And like that she might get away with the whole thing.

The salesman turned back to her. He was sulky because he felt that he had been humiliated in some way. "You want a whip, madame, to beat a *man* with?"

"Yes," she said coolly. "With a handle of perhaps twenty centimeters and a lash of about sixty. But at the end of the lash there must be that thong of knots that gives so much extra pain to the man who is being whipped."

She laughed happily as she was driven back in the taxi to the hotel. The salesman no doubt looked on her now as some sort of devil in female human form, but that didn't matter. It would in fact do him no end of good. He had been so ready to play the man-about-town act with her. In the end he had surrendered. He called the manager of his department to serve her. He himself fled in angry dumiliation.

She looked at the parcel on her lap. In it was the whip. It was not quite the sort of whip she had wanted to buy. It was not the sort their waitress of the night before had had in her hand. The manager of the department had explained politely that such whips were made especially to order. He would be delighted to order one for madame, but, necessarily, it would take a week or so before it could be ready.

In the end she had bought a murderous-looking thing that was, at the same time, a dog-leash and a heavy tapered whip. It was about three feet long and was, she decided, every bit as good for her purpose of thrashing her husband as the waitress's would have been.

One step had been taken. She had the instrument.

Next came the more difficult part. How on earth could she bring the thing up with James? *How* could she tell him that she wanted to whip him?

She remembered her decision in the store.

Just take a deep breath and say what you want to say!

Yes, it had been easy in the store—and it had also been effective. But would it be equally easy with James?

She sighed, patting the parcel on her lap. She would soon see.

James, at this moment, was lighting another cigarette in the garage to which he had taken the Land Rover for various servicing jobs. There had been a number of other people in front of him and he had had to wait his turn.

He began to think of the girl who had wanted to whip him.

Really, that was quite a thing! And she had really meant it. And, what was more, Helena wouldn't have minded. Or so she had said. But she had been tight—tight as a tick.

What a pity, though! What a hell of a pity that Helena didn't have the same perverted appetites as the waitress. To hell with the waitress! He didn't want to be whipped by *her*. He wanted to be whipped by Helena—and nobody else.

He sighed again, inhaled deeply on his cigarette, reflected that he shouldn't really be sad because his wife was not a perverted sadist. The sooner he forgot the whole thing the better.

It was a great pity, though, that he had been able to find the address of the night club.

A mechanic approached him, told him that the Land Rover was ready, and led him to the cash desk.

James drove back to the hotel making a series of solemn vows to put out of his mind for ever the new desires that had just entered it.

He parked the car outside the hotel, looked at his watch, saw that he was very late. He realised he should have telephoned. Helena would have been back for quite some time by now. She might have worried.

He took the lift up to their floor. He hurried along the passage to their room. The key was hanging on the lock. Yes, she *was* back, as he had supposed.

He opened the door and hurried in.

He came to a sudden halt. His eyes went as wide as golf balls. And his heart seemed to turn a full somersault.

Helena was standing beside the bed. She was nearly naked. She wore only the flimsiest brassiere and panties of black lace. Her legs were covered, however, by her stockings—held up by the black suspender-belt that peeped out from under the panties—and her feet were encased by shoes with very high stiletto heels. And in her right hand there was a very vicious looking whip.

For a second he felt faint. He even wondered whether he had come to the right room. He put a hand to his head.

Helena watched him carefully. His first reactions were going to be very important.

He seemed to be feeling a little faint.

She drew a deep breath. It was really all or nothing now. Let her say what she had decided to say and see what happened.

At the last moment she lost courage. "I was worried, darling," she said weakly. "Why didn't you phone?"

He stared at the whip in her hand and felt his heart turn another tremendous somersault. Dear wonderful Jupiter! She had bought, or borrowed, or stolen, a whip. And there could be only one reason...

He went up to her and took her in his arms. "And you're going to whip me for not phoning? Is that it?"

She nodded her head dumbly. He had taken the first part well enough.

He put his hand to the whip. "That's a hell of a thing, though, to be whipped with—just for not phoning!"

She looked into his eyes. "It's not just for that, Jamie. I'm like that girl last night. I want to whip you. Just as she did. Do you mind terribly?"

He felt a great peace stealing through him. He lifted her off her feet. "That is just wonderful, sweetheart. No, I don't mind. Not at all. I've longed for you to want to do it—but it seemed so impossible."

She was startled. "Since when?"

"Last night."

"Good heavens! You too!"

"Was it last night with you?"

"Yes."

They clung to each other in great happiness for a few moments, and then she drew away. "Well, come on, then," she said shakily. "If I'm going to whip you, I want to start. Get your clothes off."

He undressed himself quickly.

She said: "I must tie your balls up. But what with—and where to?" She looked round the bedroom for a firm enough fixture to tie him to. At first she could see nothing. Then the radiator presented itself to her igeniuty. It was a fairly tall wall radiator. His testicle bag could very easily be tied to one of its pipes.

But what, she thought, shall I use for string? There's plenty in the car but there's nothing up here.

She looked round the room searchingly.

Suddenly, an idea came to her mind.

"Give me one of your shoes," she said. "I'll use one of your laces."

He nodded. "A good idea. And full marks, my sweet, for cleverness. I was trying to help you but I couldn't think of anything."

She looked at him carefully. "You really want to be tied up like that?"

"Yes," he said at once.

"And you *really* want me to whip you?"

"Yes, my darling, I do."

She sighed. "This is too wonderful for words. I was going to ask you why, but let it pass. I'll ask you another time, not now."

"Good. I doubt if I could answer now."

She pulled the lace free from the shoe. "Open your legs a little." She made a loop in the lace. "Is this how she did it last night?"

"Yes, I think so."

She passed the loop over his testicles and drew it tight. "Does that hurt?"

"It does a bit," he said, "but it's an exciting sort of hurt."

She pulled on the ends of the laces again.

"Ow! he exclaimed."

"It hurts properly now?"

"Yes, it does."

"Is it still exciting?"

He considered. "Yes, it is. I don't know how—but it is. It's a sort of sweet pain—a sweet straining pain."

She felt happier than she had ever felt before in her life. "I'm so glad, darling. We're going to have some wonderful orgies together. Come on now. Move over here. I want to give you your first whipping." She pulled him near to the radiator and fastened the ends of the shoe-lace round a pipe. "I wonder whether you'll like it."

"I wonder, too," he admitted. "Theoretically, anyway, I like the idea of it."

She stepped back and raised her vicious whip. "We'll both know now." She struck him across the centre of his bottom.

Involuntarily he jumped—and let out a howl. It was a howl of awful agony. It terrified her.

She moved quickly to his side. "Oh darling, was it *so* bad?"

"No," he said, breathing heavily. "The whip wasn't at all bad. I jumped, though. I'd forgotten you'd tied me up by the balls. I nearly castrated myself."

"Oh dear," she said. "That wouldn't do at all." She untied the knot of the shoe-lace. "We don't need this, do we? I mean, since you are willing to accept my whipping, why should I tie you up?" She loosened the loop around his testicles and threw the lace to the floor. She pointed imperiously with her whip. "Go and lie on the bed. Lie down like a slave and be flogged." She drew in her breath sharply. "And *how* I'm going to flog you! I wonder whether you'll be able to take it."

He flung himself face-downwards on the bed. He buried his face into the pillow. Then he lifted it for a moment in order to speak. "What will you do if I can't?"

"Tie you up again," she said at once, moving to the side of the bed.

"By my balls?"

"If necessary."

"Suppose I scream. What then? You remember that chap last night?"

At the word itself her heart gave a little jump. "Oh darling, I *want* you to scream!"

"Good God! Do you really?" This was perhaps the sexiest of all the very sexy things she had said since he walked into the room to find her with the whip her hand.

"But not here in this hotel," she said. "So if you scream I'll have to gag you. But tomorrow in the tent..." She left the sentence unfinished.

"I can see," he said, "that we are going to avoid camping grounds from now on."

"Yes," she said, with immense determination. "From now on, the open country. Miles away from anywhere." She raised her whip, moistened her lips, and lashed his bottom. Something like a sweet electric shock struck her. She lashed again—and again—and again...

He buried his head into the pillow, biting it with his teeth. The pain was dreadful—and yet...it *wasn't* so dreadful! There was something rather exciting in it. But it was nevertheless necessary to keep biting into the pillow to prevent himself from crying out.

"And when—we're in the open country," she said, breathing heavily between each lash, "it won't matter—if you scream. It will be—in fact—so much the better."

She wondered whether he might ask her why it would be so much the better, but he seemed to be too busy biting the pillow. It was clearly difficult for him to speak.

She decided to tell him anyway.

"That is because—I want to hear you scream." She was beginning to feel tired. She must have delivered nearly twenty lashes. It was not the delivery of the lashes that had tired her, of course. It was the strong thrill that took her and shook her each time her whip flashed down across his bottom. She had not aimed at all at his back. She sensed that that might really make him scream, and it was therefore something to be kept for a camp site in the open country.

"And there in the country," she gasped, "I'll *make* you scream!"

She felt the orgasm trembling in her loins. She threw down the whip. She flung herself on the bed beside him. She said: "Turn over! Take me quickly."

She felt for his penis. It was enormous. She opened her legs, half—turned her body, guided the penis towards its destination, and gave a long-drawn-out sobbing moan as it entered her.

Once again they woke and, not knowing that the other was awake, lay silent with their thoughts for a while. This morning, though, they were in their tent.

James lay on his side—his buttocks were much too painful to lie on—and congratulated himself for having found the new address of the night club. If he had not, he thought, nothing of this new and very wonderful sexual activity between Helena and himself would have become possible. They might have gone through years of their married life—perhaps *all* of it—without knowing that the one was a sadist and the other a masochist.

And what a tremendous thrill there was in being whipped. The orgasm that followed was a lot better— ten times, a hundred times better—than the ordinary one. The ordinary one was *ordinary*. This one was ecstasy...

He wondered how many times she would whip him in the coming day.

Helena, lying awake in her own bed, was wondering the same thing. The whipping of the previous morning had been breathtakingly exciting. The love-making that followed it had been sweeter than she had ever experienced. And, all through the afternoon, as they drove on, on the next leg of their journey—she with the whip coiled on her lap—there came repeatedly to her mind the thought that she should order him to stop the car in some out-of-the-way place in order to give him another whipping. She had desisted, however. Some instinct told her that two whippings on the same day might be going just a shade too far. She had better wait till at least a night had passed.

She had needed all her determination to obey the same instinct when they arrived at the place in which they put up their tent. It was in a grove of trees, and very beautiful. They had almost missed it as they drove by. It was a good fifty yards from the road, and totally hidden by the foliage of the trees. It would make the most perfect place for a good, sound, thorough whipping. But she would wait—she clenched her fists with determination—she would wait till a night had passed.

And now she lay on her back, ready to welcome another glorious day. Rain or shine, it would be a wonderful day. It would be a day of whipping. And repeated whipping, too. There would be no need to be so gentle as yesterday.

She gave a sigh of pure contentment.

He heard her. "Morning."

She turned to him and reached out her hand. She smiled. She was always very happy in the morning. He had told her that he had never known anyone he would prefer to wake up with. "Morning, Jamie darling."

He smiled back at her. He was also pretty good in the mornings. "Sadist," he said. "Awful sadist."

"Yes," she said happily. "And I'm going to whip you a bit before breakfast. I'm going to tie you to one of the trees outside."

"It's raining."

She listened. It was true. There was the faint

sound of drizzle falling on to the outer-covering of their tent.

"Damn!" she said. "All right, it'll have to be inside the tent." She looked around it dubiously.

He chuckled. "Yes, it's a bit on the small side, isn't it?"

She had to admit that it was. It was a tent for five or six people, and so it was a very roomy affair. But she saw that there would not be much room in which to swing a whip. "All right," she said with decision. "I'll whip you outside—in the rain." Then she thought that she didn't want him catching a cold and developing pneumonia... "You can wear your mackintosh," she said, a thought having come to her. "You can strip yourself naked and put it on back-to-front. "That'll keep you dry all right—but it'll enable me to uncover your bottom every time I want to whip it."

"I don't quite get you."

"If you put your mac on back-to-front," she explained patiently, "the whole of your front is protected all the time, isn't it?"

"Yes."

"And your back is also protected—as long as you stand upright."

He looked at her curiously. He was beginning to get the idea. "Go on."

"You'll be buttoned up at the back instead of at the front."

"Yes, I see what you mean."

"But you won't be buttoned *all* the way down. Only as far as your waist. The rest will be open. So when I tell you to bend over for a few nice lashes, your mac will fall open as you bend. And I'll have you naked as I want you. And when I've finished with those few lashes you'll stand up and become covered and decent again—till I tell you to bend over again."

He looked at her in admiration. "For sheer wickedness you really do take the cake!"

She was feeling very pleased with herself too. The idea had come as a passing thought, and had developed into something quite exciting. "And every morning, Jamie darling, when we're on a private camping spot like this, you'll get up and put your mac on back-to-front.

"Raining or not?"

"Yes, raining or not. And completely nude underneath." She made her voice dictatorial, as befitted the whipper—but at the same time affectionate, as befitted the loving whipper.

"All right, awful," he said. "As you say." He pretended to be reserved in his obedience, but in fact he was extremely excited.

Her next words excited him more.

"Get up," she said crisply. "Get up now, and take off your pyjamas. And then put your mac on."

He did as she said. His mackintosh, a rubberised one, was cold but not unpleasant against his skin. He buttoned it behind his neck and just below his shoulderblades. It seemed like a surgeon's smock.

"And I'll need mine," she said.

"It's in the car." He opened the tent flap, went to the car, and found her mackintosh. It was a flimsy thing of rubberised white crêpe-de-chine. He brought it back to the tent, examining it and thinking how very feminine a garment it was. Nothing, he thought, was such a personification of sexy femininity as a woman's mackintosh of thin rubberised-silk.

As he ducked under the tent flap he saw that she had got out of bed. She was stripping off her pyjamas. In a second she stood naked. "If *you're* going to have to wear a cold mac next to your skin, I'll do the same thing—to keep you company at least in that." She turned her back to him and held out her arms.

Then they had breakfast.
Then she whipped him again.
He carried her back into the tent once more and showed her who was really the master.
Then they struck camp and continued on their journey.

For the first week Helena derived great pleasure from whipping only the backside of her husband, but slowly there grew the desire to lay her lash across his back.
"Jamie," she said one morning as they were driving along, and after she felt she had thought about it long enough, "I want to give you a *real* whipping."
A thrill struck through him. He glanced at her. "What have you been doing this last week?"
"Over your back."
Another thrill struck him. "Christ!"
"Would you mind?"
"I don't know." Theoretically, anyway, the idea was exciting. "I don't know whether I could stand it."
"But you'll let me try?"
"Oh yes, I suppose so. Try anything once!"
She looked round the countryside. They were in an uninhabited region of Turkey now. "Let's do it straight away. There are some woods straight ahead. The'll be private enough."
"Okay." He shifted in his seat because his penis was erecting.
She noticed his movement. She put her hand to his flies, unzipped them, and felt for his penis. "He's very obedient, isn't he? Always gets stiff as soon as he knows his master is going to be whipped." She squeezed the hard weapon. She was feeling very excited herself.
When they came to a halt among the trees, she got out of the car, whip in hand, and studied the situation. "Get yourself stripped, Jamie. But no mackintosh

this time. I want you completely naked if I'm going to whip your back." She took some rope out of the back of the Land Rover. "And I think I'd better tie you up."

He made no reply. He was thinking, however, that it would be better to be tied up. He relished the idea of the flogging—however painful it was going to be. But he knew that if he were not tied up he might not be able to stand still and take it. So it was better to be made quite helpless.

She tied him to a convenient tree in a simple way. She made him stand close to the trunk and hold his wrists out on the other side of it. She then bound his wrists tightly. He was totally at her mercy.

With a pounding heart she began to flog him, lightly at first, then harder and harder... and harder...

The pain was more than he had bargained for. It clawed through him, tore at him, seared him. After a dozen lashes he cried out: "Stop it, for God's sake! It's too much! I can't stand it."

She let her whip fall. She gazed at him reflectively for a moment. Should she stop? Or not?

No, she thought. This was the time to establish complete mastery over him. He was in her power. He must know it. Much as she loved him, she wanted there to be no ambiguity about the separate role of each of them. She was his mistress; he her slave.

"Sorry, Jamie," she said. "Nothing doing." She raised the whip again.

Each time she lashed she felt an unbelievable thrill of sweetness flood through her loins. It was as though the softest feather, moistened with the dew of ecstasy, were playing ever so lightly over her sexual sensory system.

Suddenly, unexpectedly, he screamed.

The scream had the effect of magnifying the thrill that possessed her. In an ever upsurging abandonment of delight, she lashed with all her force.

"Scream, my darling, scream!" she whispered breathlessly.

They reached Damascus four days later. They went to a good hotel. They thought it was time to have a proper bath.

After dinner on the first night they presented the letter of introduction which Mrs Bannister had given them in London. She had said that her friend was a powerful man in those parts. It was clear that he was immensely rich, too, for his house was like a palace and staffed by innumerable servants.

"If your car is reliable," he said, after they had discussed their route across the desert, "you should not have anything to worry about. "You have a radio-transmitter, of course?"

"Yes, sir," said James. "Short wave and powerful."

"I think you'd better give me your call-sign. I will tell my people to keep their ears open in case you do run into any trouble. I have oil depots and pipeline inspection units in quite a lot of places in the desert—within some hundreds of miles of your route."

"That is extremely kind of you," said James gratefully.

"Yes, indeed it is," said Helena. "I was always a bit worried about that. It's one thing to have a powerful radio transmitter in the car. It's altogether another thing to be certain that you can make any contact with it."

The great man laughed. "You need have no fear now. If you have a break-down my people will come and find you. But you must be patient. It may take a day or so to reach you from whichever of my units gets your signal."

Helena said with relief. "That doesn't matter at all. Just so long as they come." She had a sudden thought. "What about those nomadic tribes? The Maregs or something. Are they at all dangerous?"

"The Maregs. Are they dangerous?" He appeared to be thinking seriously. "It's difficult to say. They are not *one* tribe, of course. They are many. And most of them are harmless." He paused. "But there is one that is—or has been—a little troublesome. It has become quite rich. It sells its friendship expensively. Its friendship to the oil companies, that is to say." He reflected silently for another moment or so. "There was some fuss with a French girl who was kidnapped a couple of years ago for the harem of the sheik of this tribe. But the trouble blew over in an amusing way."

"How?" asked Helena, suspiciously.

"The French girl chose to remain kidnapped. She fell in love with the sheik."

James laughed. "I wonder whether she still is."

"Yes, I think so," said the other gravely. "My last intelligence was that she is now his principal wife. And he permits her to fly to Paris for shopping whenever she wants." He laughed too. "No, I don't think even this tribe will be any danger to you. But don't forget to give me your call sign. Just in case."

It was when they were three and a half days out from Damascus that events proved the great man to have been too optimistic.

A great cloud of dust two or three miles away was the first sign of trouble, not that this was in itself ominous. Nor was it ominous when it became clear that the dust was caused by the feet of fifty or sixty galloping horses.

It became ominous when the riders, seeing the Land Rover, changed their direction and charged towards the car, firing their rifles in the air.

James at once put his foot hard on the brake. He switched on the radio transmitter. He waited impatiently for the mechanism to warm up. "Let's send a message," he said, with forced calmness, "just in case."

"I don't like it at all," said Helena, clutching his arm. He spoke rapidly into the microphone, giving their call sign three times. The horsemen were now about half a mile away. He switched the mechanism over to "Receive." There was silence. He switched it back to "Transmit" and repeated their call sign.

"Oh God!" breathed Helena. "Make them hear us!"

As he switched back to "Receive," there came the blessed repetition of their call-sign. "Receiving you loud and clear," said the voice. "Over."

"It may be nothing," said James rapidly, "but a hell of a lot of horsemen are charging at us with their rifles blazing like mad. Our position is somewhere about twenty miles from the Nish oasis. Over."

"Twenty miles from Nish," repeated the voice. "Roger. It may be nothing, as you say, but it's as well to know. We've had orders to look after you very carefully. What's happening now? Over."

"They're getting very near. A couple of hundred yards. We'll know in a few seconds. Over."

"Yes. If you stop transmitting it means you're in trouble. And we'll come as soon as we can. But we're five hundred miles or more from Nish. Can you make out what their headgear is like. Describe it if you can. Over."

James did so, very rapidly.

"That identifies them," said the voice. "They're Maregs. Over."

"Here they are," said James, as the horsemen thundered to a halt round the Land Rover. He took hold of Helena's trembling hand. The horsemen were quite obviously unfriendly. He spoke once more into the microphone. "We're certainly in trouble. Please—" He stopped speaking as he was hit over the head with the butt of a rifle.

When he regained consciousness he found that he was lying on his back on some sort of canvas bed in a large tent. He also found that his hands and feet had been tied securely to the four corners of the bed—and he had been stripped of all his clothes.

Panic-stricken, he looked around the tent for Helena. She was not there. He was alone.

His heart sank. Where was she? What had they done with her?

He heard a step at the entrance of the tent. He turned his head.

Two exceptionally pretty girls came to the side of his bed and looked down at him. One was dark and looked as though she was of the Mareg tribe. The other was blonde. It was she who spoke, and she spoke in French.

"So you're awake at last." Her voice had a curiously ominous caress in it. "You have kept us waiting a long time."

He stared at her. "I know who you are," he said incredulously.

She was not surprised. "Most people do in this desert." She spoke with a certain pride.

"You're the French girl who—" He paused, uncertain how to go on.

"Who chose to remain in the desert," she finished for him. "Yes, that is who I am."

"Where is my wife?"

"Entertaining my lord and master." She smiled, as though at a thought which crossed her mind. "For her sake, I *hope* she is!"

"What do you mean?" He knew it was a stupid question.

She ignored it. "And now you are going to entertain us."

He looked from her to the dark girl. He sensed that he was in great danger. The memory of what the Mareg women do with knives came back to him and made him shiver.

"Don't expect her to speak to you," said the lovely

blonde. "She knows only her own language—and I don't suppose *you* can speak that. Would you like to know how you're going to entertain us?"

He met her eyes. "All right. Tell me the worst."

She laughed happily. "Oh, it's not really so bad as all that. We're going to play a game of noughts and crosses on your chest and stomach. We'd have played it on your back but somebody else has been putting too many weals on your skin. It's like a railway junction. So we'll have to play it on your front."

He swallowed carefully. "Noughts and crosses? What do you mean?"

She laughed again. "It's quite easy. We draw the lines with our whips first, and then we scratch the noughts and the crosses on your skin with the tip of a dagger."

He stared at her speechlessly.

"Of course, it's dreadfully painful," she went on sweetly, "but it wouldn't entertain us if it weren't. And you do get a reward afterwards."

"Reward?" He wondered what cruel joke this was going to be.

"Yes, I forgot to tell you. Afterwards, you'll become the personal slave of one of us two. The noughts and crosses is a competition to see which of us gets you." She looked down at him with eyes that were beginning to smoulder. "It seems that you've been whipped a great deal recently. Perhaps you like being whipped. We shall see." She drew in her breath deeply. "If I win you, I'll give you a sort of pain that you've never dreamed of. But I might also let you make love to me from time to time. And that will be your reward."

On the other side of the encampment, in a large and very luxurious tent, Helena was behaving obstinately— and very unwisely. She was sitting on a pile of cushions facing the Sheik of the trible. He was a tall, handsome man of about forty. They were speaking in French.

"You are being stupid, my dear," he said. "It would be much better to surrender yourself to me willingly."

"It would no doubt be better for *you*," said Helena. "But I'm damned if I'm going to contribute to your pleasures. And where is my husband? I demand that you tell me that."

The Sheik sighed. She had already asked the question half a dozen times. He had better tell her. "At this moment he is entertaining two of the ladies of my harem."

She felt a stab of jealousy. "Entertaining? I don't believe it!"

"Let us perhaps say that two of the ladies are amusing themselves with his company."

"I still don't believe it."

He smiled grimly. It was better for her not to know. "And now, to come back to you. Are you going to submit willingly to what I want?"

"No."

He began to feel angry. "You will regret it."

"To hell with you." Helena was not feeling as brave as she was making herself sound. She felt, in fact, very small and alone and frightened.

He clapped his hands.

Two burly servants ran into the tent. One of them held a coil of rope.

The Sheik said something she did not understand. The servants leapt upon her and tore her clothes from her body. In a moment she was naked. They seized her wrists and bound them with the rope. They threw the other end of the rope over a high centre beam that supported the canvas. They pulled on the rope till Helena was standing on the tips of her toes.

The Sheik nodded. He got up and took a short

whip from a drawer in a chest beside him. He came up close to Helena. He put his free hand to her crotch and swung her backwards and forwards. "Are you going to submit now?"

Helena could hardly speak, she was so terrified. But she forced herself to whisper: "No!" But she was beginning to agree with him that she was being stupid. Why *shouldn't* she give in, for heavens' sake? Sheer obstinacy drove her on to repeat "No," but this time it was not spoken so forcefully.

He struck her neatly across her buttocks with his whip. Then he struck her across her shoulders.

Her brain reeled with the pain. She bit her tongue to stop herself from crying out. Damn him! She would *not* let him defeat her!

He sensed what was going through her mind. He shook his head in irritation. He began to whip her in earnest. He lashed her buttocks, her shoulders, her legs, her stomach, her knees—and, finally, her breasts.

The result was inevitable.

Sobbing piteously, Helena begged him to stop.

"You'll surrender to me?"

"Yes."

He said something in his own language. The two servants released their hold on the rope. Helena slumped to the ground. One of the servants lifted her and threw her back on to the cushions. They bowed to their master and left the tent.

The Sheik began to undress himself. He gazed emotionlessly at Helena as he did so. When he was naked he lay down on the cushions beside her.

"Foolish girl," he murmured, taking her nipples between the thumb and index finger of both hands. "Lovely girl. Desirable girl. But very stupid girl." He lay on his back and drew her over him, pulling her by the nipples. "Open your legs."

Helena did as she was told. She had no more fight left in her.

She was not prepared, however, for the shameful feeling of pleasure that rippled through her as his penis slowly slid into her vagina.

James looked fearfully at his two tormentors as they took up their positions beside his bed. They each held a whip of pleated rhinoceros hide, snaky, cruel-looking, of about the thickness of a man's thumb at the handle-end, the thickness of a cigarette at the lash end, and something like a yard in length.
"We now draw the lines," said the blonde, with the same cruel caress in her voice.
"There are only four," James forced himself to say.
She nodded her head. "Yes, you are right. There are only four. But they must be well drawn. It may take ten to fifteen strokes to draw each one."
He closed his eyes and began to pray.
The whips cut into his chest, a little below his nipples. They were obviously experienced whippers for their lashes fell on more or less the same weal that had been made by the first lash. They each delivered about six strokes.
The pain was shocking. In all her recent flagellation, Helena had never hit him anywhere but on his back or bottom or the back part of his legs. These whips cutting methodically into his breast gave him an agony that made him think that at any moment he would faint.
"And now for the second line," said the blonde. She put her free hand to his penis. Under her fondling—and to the surprise of both of them—it erected. "So you're enjoying this!" said the blonde accusingly.
"I most certainly am *not!*" he gasped as the lashes began to draw a deep weal across his abdomen. But as he spoke he knew he was not speaking the full truth. The pain was too shocking for him to want anything but its end—and yet... there was a certain titillation of something like pleasure beneath the agony.

And there was a certain excitement in being able to watch the faces of the two lovely girls as they whipped...

All the same, it was murder, he thought, as he squirmed and writhed under the lashes. Oh Christ! How much longer?

It took them fifteen minutes and about sixty lashes to be satisfied with the frame of lines for their game of noughts and crosses.

The dark girl said something to the blonde, and laughed. The blonde looked at him. "Do you want to know what she said?" She did not wait for his answer. "She wondered whether you would prefer to have your penis cut off. She's prepared to let me have you without the game, if she is allowed to cut this off." She took his penis in her hands again. "But that won't do at all. If I'm going to win you, I want you to have this too. So let's get on with the game."

They put down their whips. The dark girl produced two slender daggers from somewhere. She handed one to the blonde.

"It's my go first," said she. "We tossed for it before you woke up."

She put the tip of her dagger to the top right-hand corner of the frame of weals. She applied some pressure with her wrists. She scratched a deep cross on to his skin.

The dark girl at once scratched a deep nought in the corner opposite.

James clamped his jaws together tight in an effort not to scream. He closed his eyes and counted the marks as they were scratched on him. There would be nine in all.

He was wrong. There were ten. He had forgotten the custom that the winner usually draws a line through the winning trio of marks.

The blonde won the game—and with a flourish drew this line through her crosses. "Good," she said with relish. "You are now my body servant." She looked at him seriously. "Get it into your head, will you? You're a slave now. There's no escape. You couldn't get far across the desert wearing chains, could you? And you're going to be put into chains straight away." She looked down at him appreciatively. "You're going to be quite a nice plaything, aren't you." She took his penis again. "I'm beginning to want you rather a lot."

The only thought that was occupying his mind was whether the powerful friend of Mrs Bannister was powerful enough to get Helena and himself out of this frightful situation—and if, indeed, his employees would be able to find them.

"But before I have you," said the blonde. "I'll give you a bit more whipping. I don't think you are suitably subdued as a slave yet." She regarded him pensively. "I shall begin at noon tomorrow. And I think it would be a good thing for your wife to watch."

At a minute to twelve the next day, Helena was taken to the tent in which James was prepared and ready to be suitably subdued as a slave. She was escorted by the two servants who had stripped her and suspended her from the beam the day before.

"Jamie!" she cried as she saw him tied, face up, to the four corners of the bed. "Oh Jamie..." She tried to run to him but was caught by her escorts. She struggled in their grasp. They held her fast.

A very lovely blonde was standing beside the bed. She had a long whip in her hand. "You are in time to watch something interesting," she said in French. "I am now going to reduce your husband to pulp. He must be taught that he is now a slave. And you shall watch—for you are a slave too. When I have finished, your husband shall be given some time to recover—and then he shall be required to make love to me." She glanced away from Helena and looked James in the eye. "If he can't, he shall be *really* flogged."

194

"No he shan't," said an authoritative voice at the tent entrance. The Sheik strode up to James's bed. He looked extremely angry. "Release this man at once," he ordered. He glared down at James. Then he glared at Helena. "Why in the name of heaven did you not tell me that you are under *his* protection?" And he spoke the name of the friend of Mrs Bannister as though he were some deity.

DELECTUS

"The world's premiere publisher of classic erotica." *Bizarre*.

DELECTUS PAPERBACKS

THERE'S A WHIP IN MY VALISE - GRETA X

Meet four merciless women plus one nymphomaniac. Their wanton passions leave a trail of whipped and buggered men throughout Europe. These rubber clad ladies lust for blood, and it flies! Poor Per Petersen has no idea how far these femmes fatales will take him, until they descend on his home to give him a night to remember!

"My helpless whipping boy. He has to do whatever I tell him. He has to come obediently for his regular whippings. He has to do whatever terrible things I order him to do. And he cringes under my whip like a thrashed dog. He is absolutely under my thumb, isn't he? He daren't object, he daren't refuse me anything, and he daren't run away, dare he? He is totally in my power, isn't he?"

"Wild!" *Eros*. "Top stuff!" *Loaded*. "Awesome...juicy..." *Forum*. "If you like your domination heavy this may be the book for you." *Desire*. "For men who like their women dominant and beautiful." *Paddles*.   Delectus 1995 pbk 200p. £9.99

THE WHIPPING CLUB - ANGELA PEARSON

Ms. Pearson's perverse imagination is once again given full reign in this superb novel about a select club of young women dedicated dedicated to extreme female domination. Their bizarre activities culminate in a wild party at Buckley Manor where anything and everything goes.   Delectus 1998 pbk 258p. £9.99

THE WHIPPING POST - ANGELA PEARSON

The superb sequel to *The Whipping Club* follows Rodney Pearce and other members onto further adventures in relentless female domination.   Delectus 1998 pbk 256p. £9.99

120 DAYS OF SODOM - ADAPTED FOR THE STAGE BY NICK HEDGES FROM THE NOVEL BY THE MARQUIS DE SADE

Four libertines take a group of young men and women together with four old whores to a deserted castle. Here they engage in a four month marathon of cruelty, debasement, and debauchery.

This award winning play features photographs from the London production and a revealing interview with the director.

"A bizarre pantomime of depravity that makes the Kama Sutra read like a guide to personal hygiene." *What's On*. "If you missed the play, you definitely need to get the book." *Rouge*. "Unforgettable...their most talked about publication so far." *Risque*.   Delectus 1991 pbk 112p. £6.95

DELECTUS HARDBACKS

THE MISTRESS & THE SLAVE

A Parisian gentleman of position and wealth begins a romantic liaison with Anna, a poor, but voluptuous young woman, and falls wholly under her spell. Her power is complete. There is no doubt or hesitation in its wielding. Completely enchanted we watch George descend into his own private oblivion. He is powerless to resist. The greater the cruelty and humiliation, the deeper his submission becomes. His passion to obey becomes his obsession. The perversity of Anna's nature with it's absolute domination over him, ultimately culminates in a tragic ending.

"But, my child, you don't seem to understand what a Mistress is. For instance: your child your favourite daughter, might be dying and I should send you to the Bastille to get me a twopenny trinket. You would go, you would obey! Do you understand?" - *"Yes!"* he murmured, so pale and troubled that he could scarcely breathe. *"And you will do everything I wish?"* - *"Everything, darling Mistress! Everything! I swear it to you!"*

"Sordid...gripping...extreme...highly unhygienic fun." *Fiesta*. "Anna is one hell of a woman, and The Mistress and the Slave is an S/M classic." *Screw*. "Another delectable classic for collectors of decadent erotica...it possesses an elegance rare in today's erotic prose." *Desire*. "Compelling...another gem to excite." *KPPT*. "Sadistic & unpleasant." *Headpress*. "Powerful and explicit." *Lust*. "Imperious humiliation" *Fetish* Times.   Delectus 1995 hbk in d/j 160p. £19.95

THE PETTICOAT DOMINANT OR, WOMAN'S REVENGE

An insolent aristocratic youth, Charles, makes an unwelcome, though not initially discouraged pass at his voluptuous tutoress Laura. In disgust at this transgression she sends Charles to stay with her cousin Diane d'Erebe, in a large country house inhabited by a coterie of governesses. They put him through a strict regime of corrective training, involving urolagnia, and enforced feminisation, dressing him in corsets and petticoats to rectify his unruly character. Written under a pseudonym by London lawyer Stanislas De Rhodes, and first published in 1898 by Leonard Smithers' "Erotica Biblion Society", Delectus have reset the original into a new edition.

"Frantic...breathless...spicy...restating the publisher's place at the top of the erotic heap." *Divinity*. "A great classic of fetish erotica...A marvellous period piece." *Bizarre*. "Delicious..." *Sydney Morning Herald*.   Delectus 1994 hbk 120p. £19.95

PAINFUL PLEASURES

A fascinating miscellany of relentless spankomania comprising letters, short stories and true accounts. Originally published in New York 1931, Delectus have produced a complete facsimile complemented by the beautiful art deco line illustrations vividly depicting punishment scenes from the book.

Both genders end up with smarting backsides in such stories as *The Adventures of Miss Flossie Evans*, and, probably the best spanking story ever written, *Discipline at Parame* in which a stern and uncompromising disciplinarian brings her two cousins Elsie and Peter to meek and prompt obedience. An earlier section contains eight genuine letters and an essay discussing the various merits of discipline and corporal punishment.

The writing is of the highest quality putting many of the current mass market publishers to shame, and Delectus into a class of its own.

"An extraordinary collection...as fresh and appealing now as in its days of shady celebrity...especially brilliant...another masterpiece...a collectors treasure." *Paddles*. "An American S&M classic." *The*

Bookseller. "Sophisticated...handsomely printed... classy illustrations...beautifully bound." *Desire*. "For anyone who delights in the roguish elegance of Victorian erotica...this book is highly recommended." *Lust Magazine*. "A cracking good read." *Mayfair*.

Delectus 1995 hbk in imperial purple d/j 272p. £19.95

FREDERIQUE: THE TRUE STORY OF A YOUTH TRANSFORMED INTO A GIRL - DON BRENNUS ALERA

A young orphan is left in the charge of his widowed aristocratic aunt, Baroness Saint-Genest. This elegant and wealthy lady teaches Frederique poise & manners and, with eager help from her maid, Rose, transforms him into a young woman, while at the same time keeping him as her personal slave and sissy maid using discipline to ensure complete obedience. Originally published by The Select Bibliotheque, Paris in 1921, this marvellous transvestite tale has been translated into florid English for the first time by Valerie Orpen. The story of Frederique's subjugation and enforced feminisation is accompanied by 16 charming and unique illustrations, reproduced from the original French edition.

Delectus 1998 illustrated hbk 160p. £19.95

FRIDA: THE TRUE STORY OF A YOUNG MAN BECOMING A YOUNG WOMAN - DON BRENNUS ALERA

The stunning sequel to the book above follows our hero to a new Mistress and new experiences. Translated by Valerie Orpen and due to be published in 1999.

A GUIDE TO THE CORRECTION OF YOUNG GENTLEMEN - "A LADY"

The ultimate guide to Victorian domestic discipline, lost since all previously known copies were destroyed by court order nearly seventy years ago.

"Her careful arrangement of subordinate clauses is truly masterful." *The Daily Telegraph*. "I rate this book as near biblical in stature." *The Naughty Victorian*. "The lady guides us through the corporal stages with uncommon relish and an experienced eye to detail...An absolute gem of a book." *Zeitgeist.* "An exhaustive guide to female domination." *Divinity.* "Essential reading for the modern enthusiast with taste." *Skin Two.*

Delectus 1994 hbk with a superb cover by Sardax 140p with over 30 illustrations. £19.95

THE STRAP RETURNS: NEW NOTES ON FLAGELLATION

This remarkable book contains letters, authentic episodes and short stories including *A Governess Lectures on the Art of Spanking*, *A Woman's Revenge* and *The Price of a Silk Handkerchief or, How a Guilty Valet was Rewarded*, along with decorations and six full page line drawings by Vladimir Alexandre Karenin.

A superb and attractive facsimile of an anthology from 1933, originally issued in New York by the same publishers of two other Delectus titles, *Painful Pleasures* and *Modern Slaves.*

Delectus 1998 hbk (Due July) 220p. £19.95

THE ROMANCE OF CHASTISEMENT; OR, REVELATIONS OF SCHOOL AND BEDROOM - "AN EXPERT"

The Romance is filled with saucy tales comprising headmistresses taking a birch to the bare backsides of schoolgirls, women whipping each other, men spanking women, an aunt whipping her nephew and further painful pleasures.

Delectus have produced a complete facsimile of the rare 1888 edition of this renowned and elegant collection of verse, prose and anecdotes on the subject of the Victorian English gentleman's favourite vice: Flagellation!

"One of the all time flagellation classics." *The Literary Review*, "In an entirely different class...A chronicle of punishment, pain and pleasure." *Time Out.* "A classic of Victorian vice." *Forum*, "A very intense volume...a potent, single-minded ode to flagellation." *Divinity*, "A delightful book of awesome contemporary significance...the book is beautifully written." *Daily Telegraph.* "Stylishly reproduced and lovingly illuminated with elegant graphics and pictures...written in a style which is charming, archaic and packed with fine detail." *The Redeemer.*

Delectus 1993 hbk 160p. £19.95

MODERN SLAVES - CLAIRE WILLOWS

From the same publishers as *Painful Pleasures* and *The Strap Returns*, this superb novel, from 1931, relates the story of young Laura who is sent from New York to stay with her uncle in England. However, through a supposed case of mistaken identity, she finds herself handed over to a mysterious woman, who had engineered the situation to suit her own ends. She is whisked away to an all female house of correction, Mrs. Wharton's Training School, in darkest Thurso in the far north of Scotland. Here she undergoes a strict daily regime under the stern tutelage of various strict disciplinarians, before being sold to Lady Manville as a maid and slave. There she joins two other girls and a page boy, William, all of whom Lady Manville disciplines with a unique and whole hearted fervour.

Delectus have produced a beautiful facsimile reproduction of the original Gargoyle edition from the golden decade of American erotica, including 10 superb art-deco style line drawings explicitly depicting scenes from the novel.

"Another classic from Delectus." *Eros.* "Another gem... beautifully illustrated." *Paddles.*

Delectus 1995 hbk in imperial purple d/j 288p. £19.95

WHITE STAINS - "ANAIS NIN & FRIENDS"

In *Alice* a couple spying on another couple screwing in a public park become involved in a steamy group sex scene. In *Florence*, a New York office girl enjoys sex for the first time...sleeping with two men in quick succession! In *Memories* a man recounts his youth and his teenage initiation into sex by a variety of older women.

This collection of six sensual, yet explicit short stories is thought to have been written for an Oklahoma oil millionaire, Roy M. Johnson. Anais Nin is said to have paid a dollar per page to produce typescripts of explicit erotica for his own private amusement.

This facsimile reproduction also contains an explicit sex manual, *Love's Cyclopaedia*, originally published with the stories. The introduction by Dr. C.J. Scheiner tells the story of the books first clandestine edition by New York publisher Samuel Roth during the 1940s and, all the evidence for attributing this anonymous work to Anais Nin.

"Extremely filthy...groin gripping...rampant...a great ensemble of work." *Forum*. "The highly erotic stories leave nothing to the imagination." *Marquis*. "Unique...torrid...blood stirring...a masterpiece." *Redemption (Canada)*, "Beautifully written." *Lust*. "Yet another fascinating title." *Studio*. "Sensuous sexual fantasy." *Sydney Morning Herald*. "Class stuff." *Loaded*. "A book that the serious collector cannot be without." *Galaxy*.

Delectus 1995 hbk in d/j 220p. £19.95

WHITE WOMEN SLAVES - DON BRENNUS ALERA

Set in America's deep south in the years just preceding the American Civil War this book follows the life of Englishman, Lord Ascot, and his associates in the State of Louisiana. Originally published by The Select Bibliotheque in 1910 and written by the prolific author of another Delectus title, *Frederique*, this book contains all eight original illustrations.

Delectus 1998 (Due October) hbk 270p. £19.95

MASOCHISM IN AMERICA OR, MEMOIRS OF A VICTIM OF FEMINISM - PIERRE MAC ORLAN

A French erotic classic, first published in the 1920s, by surrealist, war hero, and renowned popular thriller writer, Pierre Mac Orlan, this crafted collection of erotic vignettes provides a male masochistic odyssey through America.

Translated, for the first time into English by Alexis Lykiard, and including five J. Sonrel illustrations from the French original.

Delectus 1999 hbk 200p. £19.95

EROTICA • SEXOLOGY • CURIOSA - THE CATALOGUE

"For the true connoisseur, there is no better source." Bizarre

Delectus are the only global specialists in selling quality antiquarian, rare, and second hand erotica by mail order. Our unique illustrated catalogues are dispatched quarterly to almost 5000 customers in over 55 countries worldwide. Prices range from £5.00 to several thousand pounds representing the finest erotic art, literature, magazines and ephemera from the last three hundred years in English, French, German and Italian including large selections from Olympia, Luxor & Grove Press.

"Mouthwatering lists for serious collectors...decidedly decadent." *Risque*. "The leading source for hard to find erotica." *Screw*. "I have never seen a catalogue so complete and so detailed. A must." *Secret Magazine*. "One of the largest ranges of old and new erotic literature I have ever seen." *Fatal Visions*.

For our current catalogue, and two free back issues, please send: £3.00/$5.00. Payment accepted by cheque, postal order, Eurocheque, Visa, Delta, Mastercard, J.C.B. and Switch.

Delectus
Dept. SS.
27 Old Gloucester Street
London WC1N 3XX
England.
Tel: 0181.963.0979.
Fax: 0181.963.0502.

Mail order business only. Trade enquiries welcome.

(NOTE: Postage on books is extra at £1.35 per book U.K., £2.20 EEC & Europe, £5.00 U.S.A., £6.00 elsewhere by airmail)

Further publications are due in the next few months see our full catalogue for further details, or check our website at :
www.delectus.demon.co.uk